The Legend of Evelyn

Book 1

C.J. Kuenzli

Illustrations by Macon Bentley

www.BurkhartBooks.com

Bedford, Texas

A Note to My Children

Alleluia and Zion,

I started writing The Legend of Evelyn in 2013, five years before you were born. I dreamed of being a father and the stories I would read to you, and then one day the strangest thing happened; I began to write my own. It's changed a thousand times over from where it all began, but the one constant I've always had was my inspiration to write it for you. Now a story has turned into a series and a series into legend. As you grow up with these stories, I hope they guide you and keep you, that you'll share them with your children and your children's children. You will always be my A to Z, my first and last, my Lelu and Zizi.

I have and will always love you,

Daddy

Special Thanks:

Jeffrey "Walking Stick" Prussia,

    There are friends and then there are friends. You are the prior and the latter. Thanks for walking with me all these years to see this Legend become a reality.

Your friend,

Purple Mongoose

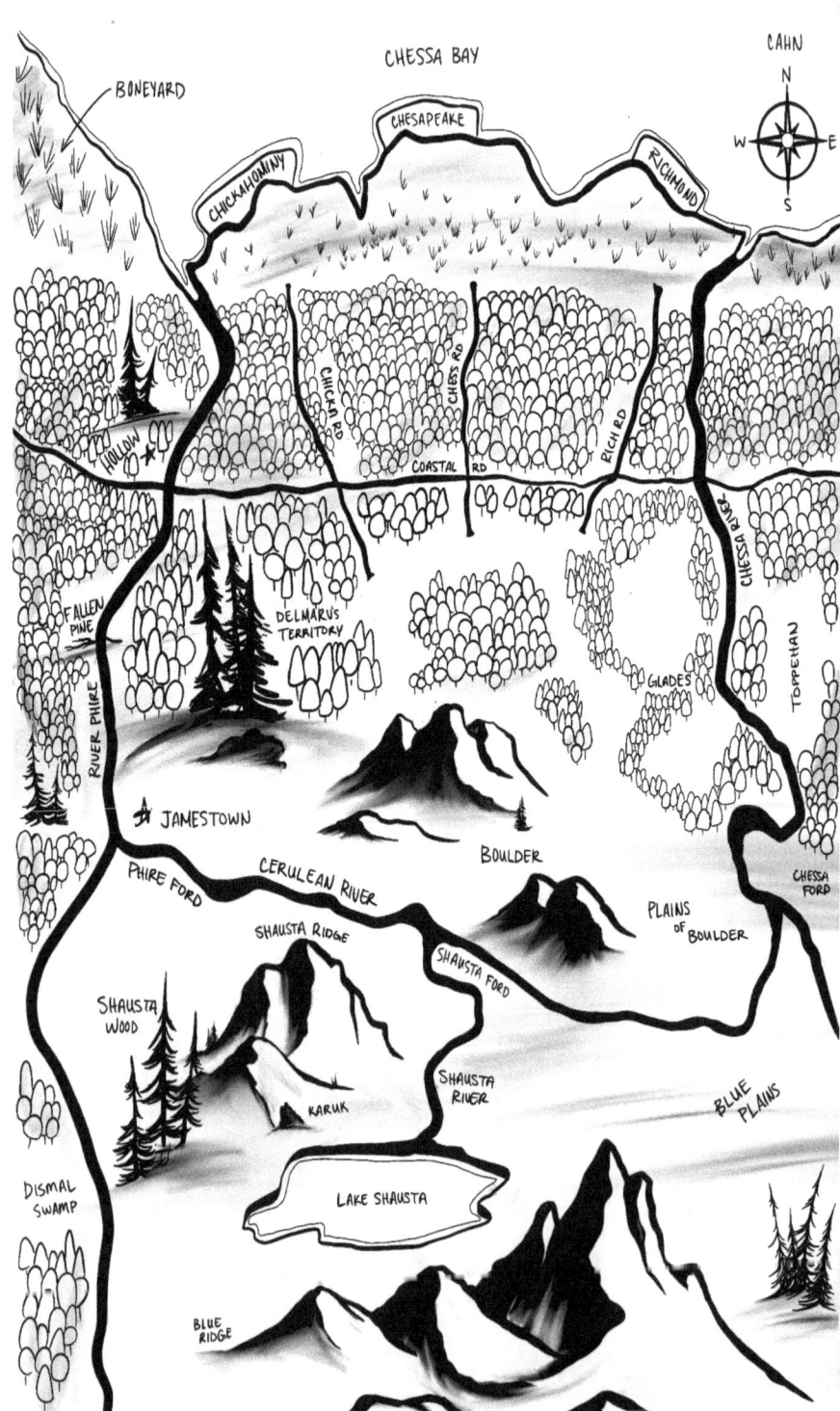

*C*ahn is in disarray. Years of war and bloodshed have ravaged the countryside.

Lutris, a brave ottermaid and next in line of otter chieftains, is fearful for her father as he accepts a meeting with their enemy, Canis.

Hyde, Lutris' father, seeks to unite Cahn under the strong bond between water dogs and land dogs; otters and wolves.

Canis, alpha of canines, better known as 'land orca' for his cruelty to otters, awaits Hyde for talks of peace. His children are not in agreement with his decision.

The fate of Cahn hangs in the balance as enemies seek counsel with one another at the ancient stronghold of Boulder.

Introduction

Before wars and bloodshed, treaties and betrayal, love and loss, was the Almighty. The absolute essence of power, life and light was the Almighty. He hovered above the corners of the world and saw magnificent potential. Within His mind, having already carved out the rest of the world, He crafted the six Covenants of the west. These land masses and waterways were made as shadows of the Realm, in which the Almighty dwells.

He placed his power, life and light into every creature He fashioned from their prospective Covenant and with each Covenant He gifted a very particular Paragon, a precious stone, one specific to its geography and inhabitants. The very stones themselves are in fact heavenly and possess the power that's revealed in the Almighty, but that same power has also been placed in each creature's life through the fragments of light bestowed upon them.

Every creature in the world carries a light inside, whether greater or lesser is based upon their use of it. The Paragon's purpose is to expose that light. The very power of the Almighty partners with every beast of the field and bird of the air and creature of the sea; yet, through the connection of these precious jewels those who possess a Paragon don't merely serve at the pleasure of that great power, but have a chance to wield it.

The Almighty looked upon the western world and smiled. "Cairn," He said, "That's what We'll call it." Twirling the Paragons in His paw, the Almighty leaned down and whispered over them. He said, "Go. And make Cairn exactly as I have shown you." With a flick of His paw the Paragons lifted into the air and went about their master's will. The Almighty returned to His throne and sat, watching His stones of the Realm working in and through and around all things.

24th Age of Cohn

I

The moon shone over the woodlands of Cahn as the night barreled onward. Hyde's army encamped on the outskirts of Richmond, the northeastern town along the Chessa Bay. Tents were filled, the watch was set, and the surround was quiet.

The young female warrior, Lutris, paced outside of her father's tent. Fuming and agitated, she wanted to go in and give him a piece of her mind, but she knew as well as anyone that wouldn't help matters here. So, she continued to pace about.

She was showing, nearly a moon cycle into her pregnancy, and nights like this didn't help her back. She unbuttoned another button from her charcoal coat, placed both paws on her lower back and stretched. Her kilt bore the pattern of her tribe and her hat was tucked, just like her sheathed knife, into her belt. Her rifle was shouldered, and her powder horn rested by her side, strapped across her chest.

She had the makings of the most fearsome warrior in Cahn and was well known as the best shot, too.

Lutris took a deep breath and walked into the tent. Hyde looked up from his maps. His eyes were hardened but peaceful as he looked at his daughter. Hyde wore a similar green jacket, though his used to fit better some seasons ago, and a blue and green kilt. His leggings were made of deer hide and were cinched at the ankle, knee and thigh with green fabric. A well-worn tam-o-shanter leaned off the side of his head like a wave caught in the middle of a crash.

"I thought you might make a trench out there with all that stomp'n about," said Hyde with a mischievous grin. Lutris took in a deep breath and gritted her teeth. "Father! Do'na go!" said Lutris, her paw smacked the desk as a look of worry ran across her face. The two otters locked eyes over the chieftain's desk. Upon the wooden table a large map lay sprawled out like drunken seaweed. Leather-bound books and the occasional scroll cluttered the makeshift war room. A chest of weapons sat in the corner, cracked open but free from dust. Light dipped from the candles that offered a flash of reflected brilliance upon the tear that ran down Lutris' face.

Lutris meant to continue, but Hyde held up a paw. Looking to the tribal elders who he had been meeting with, he said, "Until the morrow." The elders departed, leaving Hyde and Lutris alone.

Hyde, her father and chieftain of all otters, replied, "I have ta go darl'n!"

Lutris began to say, "No you ..."
But Hyde cut her off and said, "Cahn has been washed in the blood of otter and wolf alike for far too long. We must seek resolution with Canis." Hyde was a salted sea otter, grayed from countless seasons of war.

Lutris said, "You know it's a trap!"

"I know," said Hyde. "It very well may be a trap, but we must try just the same."

"Then it is folly."

"Don't give me more gray hairs than you already have, darlin'," said Hyde, with a playful chuckle.

"Father ..." Lutris began to say, but a paw from Hyde stopped her in her tracks.

"One day, me girl," Hyde said, leaning over his desk and looking her square in the eyes, "you will rule these lands and one day," he said, as he eyed her belly, "your lil pup after you. And his pups beyond him." Dipping his eyes down to the map, he added, "How long are we ta send our fellow otters into the fray? One day, as chieftess you will have ta count the cost. Not simply the cost of going ta war, but the cost of have'n gone ta war." He took the blue Paragon that hung around his neck into his paw and said, "Carry'n this stone gives us the right ta rule in Cahn, but Canis doesn't recognize it's authority; especially as long as it's in the paws of an otter. Until he possesses this it's just a gem ta him. Though, in the paws of the one who wields it justly, the whole of this southern Covenant will be at his or her's beck' and call."

Tears rimmed Lutris' sky blue eyes, as she said, "Not all in Cahn ... Not Canis and his murderous canines."

"Ay, me girl," Hyde answered, circling the desk to stand next to her. Leaning back on the table top he said, "Evil will always find its way, but we aren't here ta recognize its intent. Good beasts like you and me have been placed on this Covenant to resist evil and keep it at bay."

"Exactly!" said Lutris.

"Darl'n. Canis is not our enemy!" Hyde replied. "He is our brother. His mind has been turned for the blood lust of bygone days, yet the fact remains that he is our brother. He was made and established in Cahn as a protector over the fields and mountains and wood of the south; as we were set and established to protect the seas and rivers and coasts."

"If he's not our enemy," Lutris asked, "then why have we been fight'n him and his kind for age upon age?"

"Exactly ..." Hyde said, with a smile. This was not the intent of Lutris' question, but she had finally started to see there was no changing her father's mind. She turned around and leaned on Hyde's strong shoulder; he wrapped his paw around her.

Hyde said, "Do'na fret me girl. This darkness that we see has not yet snuffed out the light." Kissing her on the side of her head, Hyde beckoned for Lutris to get some sleep. She hugged him tight and obeyed his request.

Hyde watched his daughter leave his tent. Once she was gone he lowered his head and scanned the ground of his dwelling. Slowly he turned back to his desk, his eyes poring over the maps they'd been inspecting. His paw slid over it to the center of Cahn. "Boulder ..." he said, under his breath.

Licking his lips, the warrior otter lifted his head to the sky and whispered, "Keep me and guide me." Often of late the otter chieftain found himself conversing with the Almighty. War had worn on the brawny sea otter, and more than ever the growing darkness that was invading his shores weighed heavily on his mind.

Eying over the maps, once again, Hyde's gaze fell upon the southern mountain range of Shausta. He said to himself, "Grolg from the south ..." then swiping his eyes upward past Richmond, and toward the eastern islands of Serpens Keys, he said, "Liasis from the east." Sliding his paw left toward Chordatta, he added, "Ursus in the west." Leaning over the map with both paws clenched, the magnificent jewel fell from his tunic and dangled from his neck. The deep sapphire, roughly the size of his clenched paw, rocked forward and back as Hyde breathed deeply, suspended from its gold chain by its delicate gold setting. The candlelight was drawn to the magnificent stone, as were the otter's thoughts. Clasping his paw around the Cerulean, the Paragons name in Cahn, almost gave him a set of new eyes. The middle of the map, where he looked upon Boulder, leapt at him and reminded him of a distant memory.

"Where is it?" he asked aloud. Scanning the tent, Hyde walked about, shuffling through old scrolls and books. Frustration set in for a moment, as the object of his attention remained hidden. Still clutching the stone, he playfully asked the Paragon, "Where is it?"

A nudge from within led Hyde to pull the chest he was searching away from the tent wall where a scroll had fallen.

Taking it in his paws, he lowered the Cerulean back under his shirt, "Thank you," he said. He slid the scroll open and looked upon its inscriptions.

> "When stone of Stone walks the heights
> of Boulder and the peaks
> The dogs will bow once more to them
> that skirt the seas with ease
> Until that day when final blood
> shall stand to claim the right
> The Chieftains rule will sink in clay
> till a full and hunter moon's night

A perfect age of Chieftains strength
is him who shall arise
Though to the watchers who lose their sight
the stone won't compromise ..."

Hyde backed away from the chest as the scroll drifted from his paw and plummeted to the ground below. The well-worn paper formed back together and rolled up against the chest. His eyes followed it as his mind wandered. Long had he feared the events of the following days, though prayers to the Almighty had asked for more time, even a different way. For the first time Hyde understood his purpose in Cahn. Cupping his paw around the candle on his desk, he huffed and snuffed out the light.

2

The sun snuck up over the horizon the following morning as a small bevy of otters moved quietly out of the camp. Hyde and his twenty or so warriors lifted their heads to the sky and whispered, "Keep me and guide me". As they moved to step into their boats a gentle paw rested on Hyde's shoulder.

"I thought you might see us off," said Hyde. He imagined it was his daughter's paw, but once he turned around, he was surprised by what he saw. A solid frame of a male otter stood before him; his soft eyes often brought reassurance, even in the midst of confrontation. The river otter, Dyrk, stood eye to eye with the chieftain, though he never claimed equality with his father-in-love. The otter bowed his head, with eyes closed in respect to Hyde.

"I've come ta ask: do'na go!" said Dyrk.

"Not much of an ask," said Hyde.

"Sorry, chief," said Dyrk as he lifted his head. "Will you stay?"

"You know I can'na," said Hyde. "Does Lutris know you're here?"

"She rolled and turned all night," said Dyrk, "hoping that some form of a prayer would keep you here. All she did was keep me up."

"Then maybe her prayer was answered ... in that you are here this morn'n," replied Hyde. The old sea otter scanned the features of his river otter son-in-love. He said,

"You're a good otter, Dyrk; but you and I both know that I can'na stay."

Dyrk sighed and nodded. He said to Hyde, "Daughter like father."

"Do you think," asked Hyde, "if she were in my place that she'd do any different?"

"No, sir," replied Dyrk.

The chieftain said nothing, but smiled and motioned toward the canoes. Dyrk stood there, with a stern look crossing his face, clenching his jaw; as he watched Hyde step into one of the small boats ebbing in the Chessa Bay.

He watched them push off and paddle just beyond the port town of Richmond, where the Bay runs into the Chessa River. As they glided out of sight Dyrk's eyes lowered, he inspected the earth before him and decided to take a seat.

As the sun began to peak through the tops of the trees across the river, about an hour or so later, he placed his hat back on his head, stood and made his way back to camp along the outskirts of Richmond.

Lutris walked up beside the lean river otter and asked, "Where have you been this morn'n?" She gave him a playful wink, but he didn't see it.

"Where have you been?" Lutris asked, with a nudge.

"Just tend'n ta some family business," replied Dyrk.

Utter shock shook her bones as her eyes were fixed upon her husbands; her knees buckled and drew her to sit.

"Family business?" asked Lutris. "Then he's left already?"

"Ay, darling!" said Dyrk, as he hugged his wife. She buried her face into his shoulder.

He said, "Just give the word."

Lutris sat there, unphased, for a number of moments. She then asked, "What?"

He added, "I know you have no intention of letting him go all alone, even though he wants you ta stay put, especially in your condition."

"No I ..." she said, but Dyrk cut her off.

"Boy, you are as stubborn as your father," replied Dyrk. "He's only go'n ta Boulder, right?"

"Ay," said Lutris, while she raised a brow for her husband to go on.

"And he's gone," added Dyrk, "for a meeting, right?"

"That's because Canis told him this would be a 'peaceful meet'n.' Ha! Peaceful meet'n me tale!" said Lutris, now clenching her paws.

Dyrk snorted, and said, "If'n we go, and go now; we may have a chance to meet them there on paw."

"By the time they reach the ford we won't have even reached the outskirts of the Glades, much less the Coastal Road. We couldn't get the whole army there by then."

"Who said anythin' about the whole army?" said Dyrk. "I've got a single bevy ready and waiting. The rest of the army can catch up, but we need ta get there ta at least hold off some form of attack, if it should arise. The river twists and turns until it hits the Cerulean. A straight shot might get us there in time."

Turning to her husband she looked him in the eye and said, "Let's get go'n, then!"

"Not so fast, ma'rm!" said Tobias. The deep southern brogue seemed to rattle Lutris and Dyrk.

"Uncle!" said Lutris, "What's all this?"

"I could say the same," replied Tobias. "If'n you two are go'n after me dimwitted brother, I'm go'n ta have ta tag along." Tobias, the shorter between him and his brother Hyde, stood as tall as he could; emphatically saying that he was going. He grasped his rifle barrel like a javelin stuck in the ground and clutched his tomahawk with his other paw behind his back. His belt ran around his waist, holding up his blue and green kilt, and across his chest. His brown jacket was loose and fraying, like a fallen tree's bark. Tobias was an elder and charged with his own tribe.

Lutris started to say, "Tobias …"

"No need missy," said Tobias. "Already got a small bevy locked and loaded. They're lean and mean. Just give the word."

"Aye, uncle," Lutris said, a brief smile crossed her features.

With a whistle, Dyrk called his bevy leaders forward. Six otters stepped forward. He turned to look at them and said, "The rest of you stir up the camp. When you're all good and ready follow our trail south and west. Hold at the Glades east of Boulder. We'll send for aid if it's needed." All smiled and saluted. "Get to it!" barked Dyrk.

They turned and ran off; whistling, squeaking and calling out orders. Tobias and Dyrk rallied their own bevies, standing at the ready just outside the camp.

Lutris emerged from her tent; her tam-o-shanter tilted on her head, her necessities slung over her shoulder and across her back, her powder horn slung across her chest; with her knife slid behind her belt in front and her hatchet in back. She called out to her husband, "Set?" as she took her rifle in paw.

Dyrk called out in kind to his bevy, "Are we ready for a jolly jaunt?"

A small choir of voices replied as one, "Ah-woo!"

"Single file?" asked Tobias.

"Ay," said Dyrk. "Until we hit the glades. Then we'll fan out. Have a few of yours watch our flanks. I'll have a few out ahead. Space 'em out a bit Tob."

"Ay," replied Tobias.

Lutris lifted her arm in the air and flicked her paw forward. Southward they went, leaving Richmond and the Chessa Bay behind them. The sound of the great waters slowly dissipating as the force moved inland.

Tobias broke ranks for a moment to catch up to Lutris. He whispered to her, "Ma'rm. If'n a few of us take ta the quick march they could make the caves west of Boulder and hopefully be able ta secure an exit. If'n the situation calls for a quick retreat."

"Tobias ..." Lutris replied.

"Ma'rm ..." Tobias began to say.

"None of that ma'rm stuff, uncle," Lutris shot back, cutting him off. "We'll worry about that when we need ta."

"Ma ... Lutris," said Tobias, "we may not have time later."

"Then we'd better hurry!" Lutris said. This time she lifted her arm and swung the whole thing forward. Each otter picked up their pace.

Hyde's boats glided along the Chessa River, it was high tide, and the current was at their back. Hyde's head guard, Ptero, gave him a nod.

Hyde caught the nod and replied, "I'm right as rain, T."

"You sure chief?" asked Ptero, the speckled giant otter with a cleft upper lip.

Hyde sighed before answering. He remembered many moons back when Ptero was his confidant and friend. They had served together as elders under Hyde's father, Hars. Through thick and thin, Ptero and Hyde waged war with the wolves and foxes and coyotes of the south. When Hyde was named chieftain, Ptero was the first to congratulate him and resign as an elder. Hyde asked, "Why T?" to which Ptero said, "So, that I can be considered for your detail." That gave Hyde the greatest of respect for his friend and Ptero has been Hyde's chief guard ever since.

"Chief?" asked Ptero.

"Why do you ask?"

"It feels, if I may chief," Hyde nodded for Ptero to continue, "as if we're being baited."

"It feels that way," said Hyde, "because we probably are. Canis may have intentions of peace, but a blood lust is a hard thing ta shake."

"What?! So, you still think it's a trap? Then why are we going, chief?" asked Ptero.

Hyde sighed before answering. He said, "Because there are some things worth fighting for while other things lie outside of our control. Things that have been set in motion that not even this Paragon can divert. I'm still hopeful that Canis is truthful in his desire for peace, but I go knowing he may not."

Every creature in the boat stared at the water for a number of moments; each moment feeling longer than the other. Ptero finally raised his eyes to meet Hyde's and said, "Well. Either way, we're with you ... till the end."

"Till the end ..." echoed behind them, as the rest of the boat chimed in.

Turning around, Hyde looked deep into each one of their eyes and added, "It may be the end of this life, me friends, but only the begin'n of the next!

3

 oulder's main peak and safe haven was known to
many in Cahn as the Crown. The hill country was deserted
for many moons and laid in ruins; the Crown, itself, was
infested with webs and colonies of insects, not to mention
the occasional vagabond who'd call it home for a night or
two. Its vegetation was overgrown, and the grounds were
unforgiving.

Canis paced about the entrance of the Crown. The alpha
wolf was nearly a head taller and a shoulder wider than any
other wolf in Cahn. A tanned-hide shirt concealed most of
his scars from bygone wars. His once sleek, gray, fur was
matted and speckled with patches. A bear skin draped across
his broad shoulders, cloaking him in warmth.

The alpha of wolves paced here and there. He was
deep in thought and lost in bygone days. Many times he
had come to the Boulder country, though those times were
for other purposes. War was the way of the wolves, at least
as long as Canis was aware; what would his father think?
His grandfather? Meeting with an otter? To talk of peace?
"Otters are our enemy!" said Canis, aloud, speaking to his
fallen father. "That's what you taught me, at least. But the
scrolls ... the scrolls ... they tell a different story!"

He could hear whispers within the slanted, elegant,
doors of the great stronghold. He noticed his two offspring,
Grolg and Lupus, speaking with heads bowed low in

secrecy. Lupus, his daughter, was Canis' favored child, if he was to be honest. She was a slender gray wolf, adorned with beads, belts and fine jewelry. Her loose clothing resembled her whimsical nature, much like her mother. She flowed with a certain type of elegance in the way she looked, walked and talked. Seeing her sent Canis back to distant days with his mate.

Grolg on the other paw was a strong charcoal colored wolf. He looked every part the offspring of the alpha, but his pristine fur spoke volumes about his lack of time on the battlefield. He wore a blue coat like his father, but he didn't fill it out the same. Grolg moved about in his own inept way, never sure about himself or what he was about to do, yet when he set his mind to a task, he put his head down like a rhino, hoping to use his size to get his way.

Suspicions entered the mind of the great alpha, so he asked, "What are you two quibbling about?"

"Grolg and I were just discussing some things," said Lupus, Canis' daughter.

She embraced her father, and rubbed her neck up against his, as he said, "Discussing what?" Canis' eyes were hard and fixed upon his son.

Grolg jumped in and said, "We were just talking about the splendor of the Crown." Lupus shot a disgusting look at her brother. He brushed it off, as he continued, "This would make a marvelous outpost. Just think of it father, a stronghold on this side of the Cerulean River; it would extend our domain and give us a buffer with the otters."

"You're a fool, Grolg ..." Lupus started to say.

But Canis waved her off, and said, "Go on."

"We've been held to the south for too long," Grolg said, seeing his sister silenced helped him feel a bit more confident. "This land is budding with life and, better yet, would give us the high ground. It's time we sent a message to these water dogs, that we are the ruling class in Cahn. This land is ours. We could run the rest of the Covenant from this central location."

Canis stared off into the distance as he chewed on his lip. He breathed heavily and nodded.

"You're not seriously considering this, are you father?" Lupus asked.

"Why shouldn't he?" Grolg barked. "It's the wisest thing he could ..."

Canis cut Grolg off by asking, "Wisest?"

"Yes, father," Grolg answered, "if we were to act ..."

"Your sister was right," said Canis, "you are a fool." Grolg's eyes widened as Canis continued, "Why on earth would you take a stronghold in the center of four bodies of water? The otters are practically born in it and well crafted to navigate the bay, rivers and streams. They could surround Boulder without notice and crush any force ..."

"But we would have ..." Grolg began to say.

"Any. Force," Canis barked. "Regardless of any high ground." The old gray wolf lowered his head in frustration and sighed heavily. He went on to say, "You really haven't been listening to me, have you son?"

"Yes I have, father," Grolg snipped back.

"Then why are we here?" asked Canis.

Grolg stared at his father, a blank expression running across his face. Lupus answered for him, "To bury the hatchet."

Canis pointed a paw toward his daughter, his eyes locked on his son. He said, with an air of disgust, "Thank the Realm for your sister. You see? You haven't the faintest idea why we're here or what we're about to do. Hyde is on his way so that I can extend my paw in friendship to end this war and reopen our trade routes and strengthen our borders. Cahn, as a Covenant, is weak and anyone outside of it will think it's ripe for the taking. My father and his father before him bought the lie that we could hunker down in Cahn and war with the otters. I've seen the ships sailing in the north and the east. I've counted the tents in the west. If war were to come to our shores, now, we would be overrun. Today we're going to unite Cahn! And today we're going to make it strong!"

"What?" Grolg snapped. "I thought that was all a trap?"

"You honestly haven't listened to a word I've said for the last season," said Canis. Shaking his head, he looked up into Grolg's eyes with a tender loyalty that was edged with remorse. He said, "You leave me no choice son. I know you're the oldest and that you are in line to take over in my stead, but doing so would only leave Cahn worse off than I found it. Grolg, when we return to Shausta, you will not be ordained alpha."

Grolg clenched his jaw. He meant to bark at his father, but instead he turned and stormed off. Lupus moved to stop him, but Canis said, "Let him go." Cupping the side of Lupus' face, Canis said, "When we return home, I am going to make it known that you will be alpha."

Tears rimmed her eyelids as Lupus smiled, but then a thought jumped into her mind, so she said, "What about Grolg?"

Canis eyed his daughter lovingly and answered, "He's a kind of clever and strong as an ox, but not nearly as courageous as you, nor does he possess a measure of true strength, your strength."

"My strength?" Lupus replied, "but I'm not ..."

"Not all strength is muscle and brawn, my dear," said Canis. "I don't think I'd be saying any of these things or act like this if I was Grolg's age. I was a wicked wolf in my youth; my blood thirst exceeded that of any canine in our lineage. But now ... looking at all we've lost, your mother and your brother, I wonder if my own need for blood is what actually spilled theirs?"

Lupus lowered her eyes, "That's what angers Grolg so much. He blames the otters for their deaths. I think he misses Erold most of all."

"And he wants blood for his mother," Canis replied, "but blood will never fill that void. I'm as empty today as I was the day I killed my first beast and all it did was fuel the flame of hate inside of me; blinding me to the fact that no amount of blood could ever satisfy the brokenness within. No matter how many otters or bears or squirrels or any other beast I killed, the wounds my father left on my soul and body would never be washed away. I merely saturated the ground with innocent blood, hoping it would curse my father's bones, but I fear that I've only cursed my own."

Lupus motioned to console her father, but he waved her off. He said, "That's why we're here. I want to give Cahn a new legacy. One where peace between the water and the land can be realized in my time so that it can become a reality in yours. I'm choosing you as alpha so that these things will remain. Blood shed is not the way of the Realm, and though I may not be destined for that particular shore I pray that the Almighty will grant you and your brother safe passage because of what we've done here today."

A black wolf named Draven approached. He stepped forward. After gaining Canis' attention he said, "Three boats were spotted near the clearing in the east. They'll be here by the time the sun rises two paws from where it stands. And maybe another paw before they reach the Crown."

"With the days growing shorter we may see him in the morning," said Canis.

"Probable, sire," replied Draven.

"Well done, Draven," said Canis. "Any reports of his army with him?"

"There's been no movement along the northern woodland," reported Draven. "And no other vessels have been spotted."

Lupus asked, "Are you worried that he may have different plans?"

Canis said, "He may be stalling." Lupus looked at him with a keen eye, to which the alpha replied, "What? He's an otter, and I'm not too sure I'd believe him if he called for a 'peaceful meeting'." Turning his attention to Draven he said, "Make sure your packs stay on the western side of the Crown and keep out of sight. Leave a few lookouts in the rocks in case they try to come at us from the north or the east."

"The east?" asked Lupus.

"They were camped at Richmond but that's not to say they won't come through the Glades," said Canis. Lupus gave him a quizzical look, to which the alpha replied, "What? We're still at war."

Lupus laughed, "Make sure you know your enemy, right?"

"Exactly," Canis replied.

"I fear I may have a new one," said Lupus. With a flick of her nose, she gestured for her father to turn and look. They both saw Grolg sitting on a rock with his head buried in his paws.

"We'll settle all that when we get back home," said Canis. "In the meantime, let's get ready." The two of them walked arm in arm deeper into the Crown.

Meanwhile, along the Chessa Road, Tobias stepped forward and said, "Ma'rm ... er, Lutris. This is the last chance we have ta take the Coastal Road. The caves from the west will be lost ta us if'n we go any further."

"No, Tobias," said Lutris. "I've thought about it and I'm against it."

"Why in Cairn, not?" asked Tobias.

"Because, uncle," said Lutris, "if Canis has any force hide'n in the area it will probably be found on the west of Boulder, seeing as we were station'd in Richmond. You'd be walk'n straight into a trap."

"My," Tobias said, as he eyed Lutris, "you really have got your father's mind for tactics."

Lutris blushed, and said, "Thanks, uncle. Well, let's get go'n! Hyde must be nearing the Glades by now."

"We may miss them," said Dyrk.

"Let's hope the old dog's not in a hurry," added Lutris.

The bevies tightened their packs and were back on the quick march. With Tobias' bevy on the right flank, they would be the first line of defense should the wolves mount an offensive.

4

"Sir," Ptero said, as he pointed upriver.

A large black bear stood at the edge of the Chessa River, bo staff angled across the crook in one arm, with a shorter stick raised in the other paw, adorned with beads and feathers and tassels. He wore a red woven blanket, embroidered with more beads and jewels and other fabrics. It was a stunning piece of artwork that he wore like an old friend. Each season his mate, Loppe, would add another piece to the tunic, making it a part of their history and family. The bear stood almost a whole otter taller than Hyde, and his sheer girth made him a beast not to be taken lightly.

Hyde lifted his head and smiled, as he laughed under his breath and said, "Rappahanock!" He said to Ptero, "Pull over there."

Ptero raised a paw in the air for the three boats to make their way to the eastern bank of the Chessa. Hyde's canoe beached first, with the other two spreading out, up and down river of their chieftain. Hyde climbed out of the boat and said, "Rappahanock. And what brings the great bear of the east to the river's edge today?" The salted beard of the sea otter pulled back as he smiled even wider once the black bear approached.

"This bear could ask the same of the wise chieftain of the southern covenant," replied Rappahanock, in his precise and thought out way; his voice rumbled with a sort of thunderous respectability as he spoke. "What brings you this far south on the east river?"

The two beasts clasped paws and hugged one another; Rappahanock tapped the back of the otter's head with his prayer stick. "You always do that," smirked Hyde.

"We all need prayer, brother," answered Rappahanock, "especially when we're on the Almighty's business." Hyde gave him a quizzical look, to which the great bear replied, "Not all things have been made plain, but not all things have been hidden. Come, you and your friends, let us sit a while."

"Wish that we could," replied Hyde, "but we are en route ta Boulder."

"To meet with Canis," said Rappahanock.

"Ay," answered Hyde. "You object?"

"What has been revealed to me is but a shadow of the full intent of these days," said Rappahanock. "I do not warn against your going, for I feel the nature of this assignment is noble. But ..." The bear paused a moment.
Hyde asked, "But what?"

"There's a growing darkness stirring behind the clouds, not visible but present," answered the bear. "I fear it is lurking in the shadows for one who is not ready to resist it."

"For me?" asked Hyde, but Rappahanock shook his head. "For Canis?" again, the bear shook his head. "For who then?"

"Come my friend," Rappahanock pleaded gently, "come and sit a while ..."

"Brother, if'n we had the time," replied Hyde, "I'd sit with you fer a season ta find out all that's been revealed. But we need ta make the peaks of Boulder tonight."

With a nod Rappahanock accepted the kind dismissal, but he did say, "If you permit me, I shall give you one word of warning for your journey?" The otter nodded, as Rappahanock continued, "Though it is possible at this point that any counsel that I give can sway the events either way." Hyde gave a nod asking for the wise bear to continue, to which he did. "The who has not been revealed but the road has been set before you. The Almighty has purpose for you to ascend the hill to the Crown, so, I will continue to offer prayers on your behalf, but my word of warning to you is this: ascend the hill tomorrow at dawn. Preferably after dawn, but dawn nonetheless."

"What have you seen, my friend?" asked Hyde. Rappahanock answered, "It's not that I've seen, but what I have felt. Like the feeling an old wound gets when a great storm is brewing on the ocean. How torrential winds begin to howl, just before the showers pour. I feel that there is a delicate shadow hovering over the Crown tonight, and it best, with the sun already going down, you give that cloud some time to dissipate before engagement."

"Is it possible that by waiting," asked Hyde, "that it may strengthen in our absence?"

With a smile, the great bear chuckled and said, "Anything is possible, my wise young friend." Rappahanock sniffed the air and searched the sky. Turning his attention to the trees behind him, the bear smiled and said, "I remember planting these pines. Never in my wildest dreams could such a small seed one day become such a wonder ..." The bear looked up and examined the splendor of the wood.

"Spit it out, you old snort," said Hyde, with a chuckle.

The bear spoke again and said, "I hope you won't find me indignant, but given the late hour and the journey that is yet to come, why not rest here? I can provide food enough for you and your warriors, grant you shelter and peace of mind as you rest. Hyde, my friend, it would honor me so if you would accept my invitation."

The burly sea otter cracked a smile, and replied, "I guess there's no escape'n what's already been set in motion, is there?"

"I've yet to find a way in all my long seasons," answered Rappahanock. He raised his brows, in order to hear the otter's decision.

"I suppose we can head out earlier in the morn'n after a good night's rest," said Hyde. "We'd be happy to oblige." He turned to Ptero and said, "We're camp'n here for the night. Have them gather their things and stow the boats. Set the watch ..."

"No need for a watch," said Rappahanock, as he interrupted Hyde, "I have some already in place." The black bear raised his prayer stick into the air and gave two deep, guttural, grunts. Two more grunts echoed around them. The otters spun here and there to see black bears peering out of the wood up and down the banks of the Chessa, with a few even standing opposite the river. As Rappahanock lowered his stick the bears retreated back under cover.

"You know," Hyde said to Ptero, "for be'n giant balls of fur, they're surprisingly nimble."

Ptero chuckled as he replied, "I suppose their be'n the size of trees helps them ta blend in."

Rappahanock added, "A restful spirit, even in the presence of danger, makes a sizable difference in one's ability to blend in with his surroundings. Fear and exasperation cause a beast to stick out like a sore paw."

Hyde smiled and nodded. He said to Rappahanock, "Then it's a good thing we get to learn of this rest tonight in your humble abode."

Ptero stepped forward and reported to Hyde, he said, "Packs are shouldered. Boats are stowed. Ready when you are, chief."

Hyde nodded and said, "Rappahanock. At your leisure."

The great bear took a step back with one paw, opened one arm and gestured with his prayer stick. He said, "Right this way, Hyde." The two friends walked side by side as they entered into the thick, green wood of the east. They left the Chessa River behind them. It was quiet and serene, but it was watched.

5

They walked deeper and deeper into the wood, a well-worn path led them to a cluster of trees near the edge of a small hollow. The forest was alive with bird songs as other woodland creatures hopped to and fro throughout the wood. Hyde's crew looked around in amazement as Rappahanock raised his paw for everyone to halt. The black bear lowered his prayer stick over his mouth, signifying they all should remain silent, then he motioned for them to follow him.

Instead of walking into the clearing that lay ahead of them, Rappahanock gestured for them to follow him over the inconspicuous path to the right. Stones were scattered in such a way as not to draw attention to their placement or direction, but they were spaced out perfectly for a black bear to walk along. The otters didn't find it so easy, for they had to leap from one stone to another.

Slate, a lean female otter with a nubby left ear, began using her rifle as a stave to cross from one stone to another. She'd reach the butt of her rifle as far as she could and pole vaulted across the divide with ease. The other otters looked wide eyed at each other, chuckled quietly and followed suit.

Rappahanock saw the playful otters making a game out of the difficult crossing. With a smile he continued to show them the way.

As they reached an enormous oak tree situated among a forest of conifers and spruces the black bear took a step off of the last stone and walked around to the other side of the tree using a variety of mature and exposed roots. The otters followed suit, as they did before with the stones, until they came upon a grand root-archway at the base of the tree. Rappahanock took his bo staff and rapped it upon the archway. A moment or so later, an answer was made with a similar sound, but this time from within the tree.

Rappahanock smiled and gestured, as he did before, for the otters to enter as a doorway opened within the archway of the grand oak. The door raised from the bottom up, as two black bears on the underside of the tree lifted the secret door. The otters made their way into the entrance and gathered on the other side. Once Hyde and Rappahanock passed the threshold, the two bears closed the door behind them.

The door thudded shut, and Rappahanock said, "I apologize for the secrecy. Few in the eastern wood know of our presence, and even far fewer know of our whereabouts. This is one of four entrances into Toppehan."

Ptero leaned over to Hyde and said, "Toppehan? I thought that was an old mum's tale?"

Rappahanock gestured for Ptero, and others, to turn around to walk down the sloping and narrow corridor. As they did it opened up into a grand and illustrious cavern. Root systems ran here and there along the ceiling, acting like beams for the underground dwelling. Roots also welled up out of the floor and were used for seating and partitions as more roots ran through the dirt walls.

Hyde ran his paw along the engravings of the underground branches. Each carving told a story of Cahn. Bears, wolves, otters and the like could be seen etched into every root and bulb.

The otter chieftain was one of the few in Cahn that was ever given entrance into Toppehan. Having returned to the grand stronghold of the east Hyde looked all around and said, "I can never truly remember the splendor of this great house, then when me eyes look upon it I can barely forget a moment."

Rappahanock smiled and watched as the otters spread out to view the spectacle of his home. "It's often through the eyes of newcomers," said Rappahanock, "and even old friends, that I gain another appreciation for all the Almighty has bestowed upon us."

Ptero replied, "Mighty are the blessings upon you and those of Toppehan!"

Rappahanock patted Ptero on the back, and said, "Such are the blessings upon each otter when you skirt the waterways of Cahn. Welcome to the dirtless rivers of Toppehan. It's caverns and corridors hold the expanse of our beloved hallow and beyond. Do you remember the clearing you saw before we took the stone path?"

"Ay," replied Ptero.

"That hollow is now directly above," said Rappahanock.

Ptero looked up in pup-like wonder, "Really?"

"Toppehan is the hollow," replied Rappahanock, "yet those who know not of the true hollow beneath will only ever see the brief clearing in the trees. Leaving it as a, what did you call it? A 'mum's tale?'" He and Ptero chuckled as they walked together.

Ptero said, "I feel that I should be overwhelmed by it all, but the very sights and smells and feeling of it only give me a sense of home. A sense of peace."

"Welcome to Toppehan," said Rappahanock. "Welcome home." Spreading his arms out wide, the black bear invited Hyde and his otters to join him at his table. There were a number of tables intricately placed around the hollow, the one Rappahanock led them to, was the center table. It was long and wide, with tall benches along its sides. Each bench could hold a bear or three, depending on their size, but the otters could sit four or six on each, depending on their size.

Once every-beast was seated, Rappahanock raised his stick into the air and said, "Almighty! We welcome You in this place! We know that Your presence is always with us, yet we make ourselves aware of You as You make Yourself aware to us. We welcome You because You are worthy of such. We ask that You bless this table, the food upon which we will eat and the company with which we will share. We give over to You our worries of tomorrow, for we cannot even put into words what might and might not happen. As for tonight, we give You access to our table as You give us access to Yours. In Your presence we pray these things ..."

A chorus of voices shouted from all over Toppehan in reply, "Selah!"

"Selah?" asked Ptero.

Hyde smiled, as he leaned in to answer Ptero. He said, "It's how they end their prayers to the Almighty." Rappahanock chuckled and said, "Well, it's how we finish that portion of our prayer, but extend it into our lives from then on. Selah. It means 'that we should sustain these things'. It finishes the formality of the prayer, as it were, but invites us to stay within that prayer as best we can until the next."

Ptero nodded as he allowed the meaning of the word to roll around his heart, "Selah. I like that."

"Should we start using it?" said Hyde, as he nudged Ptero. "By all means," replied Rappahanock. "It's not ours to keep, but to share. It's a word of the Kingdom ... that is the Realm. Use it and spread it around Cahn as best you can." Noticing the food that was approaching the table, the bear said, "Come, the time for talking and tales is before us, let us join now in feasting and celebrating."

6

Large cauldrons of piping hot stew were lifted and spread out along the table. Rolled up hush puppies were stacked in wooden bowls next to heaping towers of smooth churned honey-butter. Bowls for the stew were dispersed and spoons were taken. Rappahanock said, "Consider this your home. If you need to stand on the table to reach the stew, by all means, take and eat." Hyde and Ptero climbed onto the massive table to help ladle out the aromatic contents of the cauldrons.

"Hmm," said Hyde as he caught a whiff, "is this crawfish stew? And hush puppies?" Rappahanock nodded, as Hyde added, "So, you knew we were coming?"

"It may be why I insisted that you come," said Rappahanock. Slate asked, "You made this just for us?"

Rappahanock smiled as he answered, "Let's just say the Almighty has a way of lining up the right meal for the right guest on the right day."

"Toss me a pup!"

"I'll take two!"

"How many can I have?"

Hyde dished out the stew as Ptero tossed hush puppies left, right and center.

Laughter ensued as otter and bear sat together in the center of the large cavern. Joyful sounds of stories mixed with the scent of freshly curated stew and brewed coffee, each weaving their way in and out of the grandiose root systems of Toppehan.

Slate leaned over and said, "Oy, Mik."

Mik, a larger-than-life giant otter, looked out of the corner of his eye and growled, "Oy."

"Can you ladle me some of that stew?" asked Slate.

"Mmhm," replied Mik. He took Slate's bowl and scooped it into the cast iron pot. "Here," he said.

"Thank you, kindly," said Slate. "Next time, can you hold down the conversation a bit? You long winded river rat." Everyone chuckled. Everyone but Mik, who tipped the stew over into Slate's lap.

"Ahhh!" screamed Slate. "You monster! You ruined it!"

"It will wash out," replied Mik.

"Not me clothes," said Slate, "you ruined some perfectly good stew!" Laughter lit up the table as Mik took his own bowl and plunged it into the stew. He chased her with it. As they ran, Slate shouted, "Don't you go an' ruin another!"

The laughter was like a healing balm over the small bevy of otters. The events of tomorrow weighed heavily on every heart, but the weight was lifted with each taste of stew and every belly laugh. The otter chieftain smiled as he watched Slate and Mik chase each other like a couple of pups, glad to see the wisdom of youth still alive in each of their souls. "Hmm," he laughed to himself, "If only life was able to stay like this ..."

"It is," said Rappahanock.

"How?" asked Hyde. "When life as we know it is filled with war and bloodshed?"

"Until our next life," answered Rappahanock, "I'm not so sure we can avoid bloodshed. Look at these crawfish. We don't pay them any heed as we devour them by the mouthful, and yet we have possibly slaughtered hundreds, if not thousands of them, within this meal alone." Hyde gave a hearty laugh, as the bear continued, "All joking aside, bloodshed has been inherited among the beasts of this world until we are fully redeemed; until darkness is fully snuffed out. Until then, it's in moments like these that we must remember to check the weight of those battles at the door and invite ourselves to slip back into the ways of the young. To carry war on your shoulders all the time is not wisdom, but a prison. We must still keep vigilant, but in spaces like these we must let our hearts breath with mirth, and gain what strength we can for the moments that will be needed ahead."

"So, we won't speak of tomorrow?" asked Hyde.

"We are speaking of it now," answered Rappahanock. "Through food and story; even through those two chasing each other about. As the time comes, and the Almighty reveals it, we will discuss that which needs to be. Until then, just like our time on this good earth, we shall enjoy the moment as it rests before us."

"Not rushing the moment at paw ta get ta the next," said Hyde, "but taking the moments as they come?"

The great bear nodded his head slowly. He took a sip of his mug and said, "That's it. Plans and preparations are necessary, but if more beasts of the field and wood took time for themselves and others in their care this Covenant would be a might better off."

"How does one plan then?" asked Hyde.

"The plan?" answered Rappahanock. "The plan is to be ready at all times for anything, but able to rest in the times of nothing. The seasons teach us that. Spring is for preparation. Summer for growth. Fall for harvest. Winter for resting. Interestingly enough, I've found that each of us has seasons of the soul. Times of our lives where we prepare, grow, harvest and rest. The duration of each is never as long or short as the previous season or even the cycle; but the seasons play out in this way in each of us. Tonight, though you may be marching to the season of either preparation or harvest between you and Canis, we are found in a short season of winter."

"How so?" asked Hyde, a few other otters now listening in on the conversation.

"Winter is a bare, but fruitful, time," replied Rappahanock.

"Fruitful?" asked Ptero, "How can winter be fruitful? When everything seems dead."

"Take the oak we passed under earlier," said the bear. "Even in winter these roots, that you see here, are budding and full of life. Though the branches bear no fruit, the fruitful season to come is being harnessed within its bark. It's the way of the Almighty. Seasons of work. Seasons of rest. Rest is neither stopping nor nothing. Rest is simply a season of potential being built in anticipation of spring."

Otters around the table found themselves deep within the recesses of thought as the simple explanation washed over their hearts and minds. Hyde said, "So, ta miss this opportunity in anticipation for the next means that we might lose the chance ta see spring? Even summer?"

"It's all in how you look at it," said Rappahanock. "Tomorrow could be the beginning of the groundwork for sustained peace in Cahn, or it could be the fruition of it. That is yet to be seen, and only enjoyed in its proper time and season."

"What of the warning you gave earlier?" asked Hyde.

"Warning? Oh, you mean the cloud?" asked Rappahanock. Hyde's nod allowed the bear to answer. He said, "When we try to extend the seasons from passing, we end up burning out what the Almighty has allotted for us; allotted in due season. The beast or beasts that are living in seasons past try to take matters into their own paws to eliminate change. As you and I both know, this is impossible. The very seasons themselves are evidence of change, revealing to us that control is beyond our grasp. If any control is to be held, it is in the knowledge that we cannot control the changing of seasons; both in the creation or within the created. The cloud, that I mentioned, is one that hopes to extend that which the Almighty is calling into extinction. Our prayer must be that the Almighty would reveal this nature of seasons to this creature in order to loosen the grip of control from their lives."

Ptero added to the conversation, somewhat out of breath, by saying, "So, essentially, we are all in each season with different situations?"

Hyde looked at him and asked, "What do you mean, brother?"

Rappahanock smiled, recognizing the truth the otter had spoken, as Ptero continued, "Tonight we are in a winter season of rest and at the same time a summer season of growth. It's even possible that each of us are all in a different season as you speak, Rappahanock, because some of us are just waking up, spring, to this idea, while others of us may be growing in our knowledge of it or even harvesting something we've been growing for years. When it comes to tomorrow, we're stepping into a possible harvest season; where we experience the measure of peace we haven't tasted before. While at the same time it could be a spring season for Canis who's not ever dreamt for peace in his life."

"Well said," said Rappahanock.

"I'm go'n ta need another helping of stew ta wrap my mind around that one," laughed Hyde.

"You're go'n ta need another belt to wrap around your middle if'n you have another helping of stew," added Slate. Laughter exploded around the table as Hyde held a paw to his stomach. "Maybe two belts!" he said.

As the giggles died down, Rappahanock looked at Ptero and said, "You are wise beyond your season, my friend. You are correct, by my understanding, each of us is in a different season with each and every situation we come into contact with. I'll remind you; it is not our job to understand it all or control it, but to go with the seasons as you would go with the tide."

Turning his attention to the rest, Rappahanock said "May we relocate to the fire, where there is more comfortable seating?" Hyde lifted his bowl, took another piece of bread, and followed the great bear toward the cushioned armchairs while others followed suit; some filled their bowls with stew while others filled their mugs with coffee. "Oh! If I had known," said Rappahanock, "that we were still feasting I wouldn't have ..."

Hyde interrupted his friend, and said, "We may have another nip or two between now and later. Don't mind us."

Rappahanock chuckled, as he said, "The appetite of otters ..."

"The appetite for crawfish!" replied Hyde.

"Ah, come my dear," said Rappahanock as his face lit up while he raised his paw to a beautiful female black bear, with speckled, tan, features scattered across her face and neck. The emerald-green tunic around her shoulders was as magnificent as Rappahanock's, though she wore it with a type of humble sophistication. She brought a new clay pitcher of coffee and placed it on the table. She stepped forward as Rappahanock wrapped a paw around her shoulder. He said, "Hyde, you remember my mate, Loppe?"

"Ay," replied Hyde, "of course I do. How are ya, lovely?"

"Fine, chieftain Hyde," said Loppe. "We're so blessed to have you in Toppehan, once again."

"None of that chieftain stuff," said Hyde, with a chuckle. "You know better than that! Where's that daughter of yours?" Like a thunderbolt, another female black bear came running up behind Hyde and scooped him up into her powerful paws. As she lifted him into the air Hyde shouted, "Watch it!"

"Not the stew!" shouted Slate, to which the otters roared in laughter once more!

Balancing stew in one paw and coffee in the other, Hyde tried to peer over his shoulder to see who had absconded with him up and off of the floor. With a sense of mock horror, he said, "Who is this? Unpaw me at once! I demand ta know who's interrupt'n me stew!"

"It's me, uncle Hyde!" she said.

"Penel?" replied Hyde, "Is that you?"

With that, Hyde was lowered to the ground where he could spin around and look her in the eye. Her deep brown eyes were framed in the same light brown speckling as her mother. Her magenta tunic caused her fur to shine and her eyes to dazzle. She was Rappahanock and Loppe's only offspring and though her parents ruled over Toppehan, she never used that fact as something to be lorded over any other beast. She served Toppehan, and Cahn for that matter, with the same sense of dignity that her father and mother used for generations.

Hyde pulled back and said, "My, what a beauty you are me dear! More and more the spit'n image of your mother!"

Penel blushed, as best a bear can under all that fur, as she lowered her nose and smiled. She said, "Oh, uncle! Mother's beauty far exceeds any in Toppehan!"

"Perhaps, most in Cahn," said Hyde, "but me dear, it may be safe ta say that you're give'n her a run for her stew!"

Penel blushed again by lowering her nose as she smiled. She said, "It's good to see you, Uncle Hyde."

Rappahanock chuckled softly to himself, and said, "Come. Let's have a seat."

Rappahanock smiled at his wife and daughter, marveling at their beauty and grace. He then turned to Hyde and said, "May I?" as he pulled his pipe from his pouch that hung off of his neck.

Hyde answered, "By all means. I'll join you."

Rappahanock smiled, and began pawing at a smaller pouch, filled with cured leaf. He clawed the tobacco into his pipe, stuffing it quite full. Once completed, the bear took a long twig and reached it to the edge of the fire. When the end was lit, he lifted the torch just above the bowl of his pipe and breathed the flame into the leaves. Smoke began to billow from the bowl and seep out of the edges of his lips. He tamped and lit again. Then he shook the flame from the twig. Now that the pipe was lit, he leaned back in his chair, puffing a slow, even, drag. He released a cloud of smoke and licked his lips, tasting the flavor of leaf and honey, with a slight hint of coffee. "Hmm," he said, "this may be the best cure of the season!"

"Have you been cure'n your own leaf?" asked Hyde.

"Yes," said Rappahanock, "this is our fifth crop and only our third cure this year, I think. This is by far my favorite. Would you and your otters like some? We have some loose leaf for pipes and some wrapped in cigars."

The otters heads bobbled forward and back at the generous request. Rappahanock raised his paw for his cedar boxes to be brought. Two bears carried and opened the boxes to reveal stacks of cigars and pouches of pipe tobacco. Rappahanock said, "Take a pouch of leaf or a few cigars. Help yourselves. What's mine is yours. We have plenty for all."

Pipes were stuffed and cigars were nipped. Twigs were lit and smoke was kindled. Each beast that partook in the cured leaf smelled and tasted the leaf to their enjoyment. Hyde said, "This is quite lovely, but tell me friend; how does the Almighty look upon such practices?"

Rappahanock puffed on his pipe and said, "Well," blowing a ring of smoke, "He gave us the leaf and the skill to cure it. I also like to believe that the throne of Him, on High, is covered in billowing smoke; we here are joining Him in like fashion!" They all joined the bear in a good laugh. He pointed his pipe at those sitting around him and said, "But, if it ever gets to a point where it becomes a need instead of an enjoyment, it may be time to take a break from the leaf. Just like all things, moderation is the key." Everyone nodded at the wisdom Rappahanock shared.

Many sat back deeper into their chairs as they enjoyed the honey and coffee infused tobacco. He saw Penel approaching with mugs of hot coffee and bottles of honey nectar. He said, "Ah, here's more coffee and some of our June Moon. It's an aged nectar. We just tapped a new cask this last week. It's been aging for a great many moons. I sampled some just last night ... and the night before. Well, to be honest I've had a nip or two nearly every night since I tapped it. Hmm, hmm, hmm. It has a sweet pallet to it with notes of honey, fruit and nut. To say it complements the leaf is an understatement. Please take and enjoy."

Drinks were poured. Logs were added to the fire. Once the atmosphere was stilled and full, with the smoke dancing along the roots above, Rappahanock cleared his throat. Hyde gathered the time for feasting and celebrating had come to an end, and that the time for discussion had peaked. He said, "So, Rappahanock, may I ask you a question?"

"I wish you would, my friend," replied the bear. "I wish you would."

7

Across the Chessa River, quite some distance away on the northern border of the Glades, Lutris and her otters were bedding down for the night.

"Scouts are set on the edges of the Glades, river and road with another party just north of us," said Dyrk. "If'n a wee canine comes 'round the corner, we'll know as quick as we spot a trout in a creek."

Lutris nodded, and said, "Good. We need ta gain the threshold of Boulder about sunup if'n we hope ta make it there in time. But I need to shut my eyes for a bit."

"We've been running hard all day," said Dyrk, "you deserve a bit of shut eye. Do you mean ta cut them off south of Boulder? Or come up the east side and meet them?"

"If'n we planned ta cut them off south, we'd have ta have sent a party earlier this morn'n," answered Lutris, "that's hope'n, and I'm hope'n something fierce, they waited for morn'n ta climb the wee hill. But there's no tell'n where they beached their canoes ..."

"So," said Dyrk, "we come up the east side?"

Sighing, Lutris said, "We can use the wee clump of trees as cover, you remember? The ones just off the Glades?"

"Ay," said Dyrk, "that's a jolly jaunt from here though. When we get there we'd better move. The sun will be at our backs and that may lend an able paw."

"Ay," answered Lutris, "A few of us can sneak up the hill and see what needs ta be seen once we reach the grove."

"Us?" asked Dyrk.

"Ay," said Lutris, "I'm not leave'n me father up there with the land orca."

"But you're with pup?" said Dyrk, full of wonder.

"Don't you think I know that?" asked Lutris.

"Fair enough. But have ya thought ta ask yourself," said Dyrk, "what ta do if'n Canis was tell'n the truth?"

"That's one less dead wolf, I guess," replied Lutris. She looked Dyrk in the eye and said, "Grab some shut eye, we're gonna need it in the morn'n."

"Aye, ma'rm," said Dyrk. He dodged as Lutris attempted to smack him. He tipped his bonnet to her and said, "Ma'rm!"

Lutris laughed and shook her head. Dyrk laid down next to her. Once he was good and settled, she delivered another smack. "Oy, what's that for?" he asked.

She laughed and said, "Insubordination!"

"Insubordination?" asked Dyrk, wide eyed and mystified. "I'll show you insubordination." The strong river otter took Lutris into his arms and kissed her. He kissed her hard and good.

Lutris pulled back, "I could have you flogged for such reckless behavior!"

"For you my dear," replied Dyrk, "I'd gladly take it!"

Lutris smiled and pulled her husband back in for another kiss. When she was done she said, "Now. Get a move on, you rebellious welp. Back ta your tent with ya!"

"Aye, ma'rm," said Dyrk, as he smiled and rolled his eyes playfully. He stood up, walked out of the tent and then entered again. He said, "And where is my tent exactly?"

Lutris rolled her eyes and said, "Come to bed you goon."

"Yes, ma'rm"

Dyrk laid down and the two otters cuddled closely and held each other tight; whispering sweetly to each other.

Most of Hyde's otters had drifted off to sleep. A mixture of smoke, fermented nectar, long conversations and a peaceful fire caused heavy eyes to fall with ease. Hyde and Rappahanock were the only two left awake. The great bear returned from clearing the table and sat next to Hyde. The sea otter was deep in thought, his eyes reflected the dance of flame upon scorched wood. Rappahanock breathed deep, and said, "There are worse ways to spend an evening."

Hyde looked around the room. Bears were huddled up in their corners, his otters were sprawled all over their armchairs, and a few candles held just a moment or two more light before burning out. The sea otter nodded, "What a night, indeed."

"Where are your thoughts, my friend?" asked Rappahanock.

"Scattered at best," replied Hyde, "but peaceful at worst."

The black bear nodded, and said, "Not a terrible place to be."

"Not at all," replied Hyde, "clearly we all needed a peaceful night."

"I've not seen a response like that in many years," said Rappahanock. "It's beautiful to see what good food and fellowship can do for the soul. To see all of your warriors sleeping like pups is such a precious thing. I wonder when it was the last time they slept so deeply?"

"Longer then I care to imagine," said Hyde.

"And yet," replied Rappahanock, "you seem to be more awake than you were earlier."

"I am rested," said Hyde, "tonight was like a soothing balm over my soul. I could stay awake for seven days and not grow tired after this." The otter turned his head toward his friend, as he said, "I'm sorry that it's taken this long for me to return. In the chaos of these many moons, I have forgotten how to drink deeply of life and so I have stayed away. Some because I do'na have time. Mostly because I do'na make time."

"No apology is needed my friend," said Rappahanock. "You came at exactly the right time and it is our privilege to have hosted you. I hope that, when the time is right, we will be able to host you here again."

"I fear that this may be the last time I'm to visit Toppehan," said Hyde. His nose began to quiver slightly as his eyes welled gently with tears. Rappahanock didn't say anything, but he did place a paw on his friend's shoulder as he continued. The sea otter said, "I found an old scroll in my tent the other night. It reminded me that the chieftains rule would 'sink in clay' until a hunter's moon night. I know we haven't had such a moon in these parts for an age ..."

"But that's not what's bothering you," asked the bear, "is it?"

"I think it is," answered Hyde, "I'm worried that the chieftain's rule will end with me in the clay tomorrow. And that there's nothing I can do ta stop it."

"The events of tomorrow are yet to be seen," said Rappahanock. The bear stood from his chair and knelt before his friend, resting both paws on the otters' shoulders. Looking Hyde square in the eyes, he said, "This burden is not yours to carry. The Almighty trusted you with that scroll because He trusts you with the revelation that it carries. Now. Here and now. Here and now is the time for you to live. The day that you move on to see the Almighty has not yet come, so here and now rest my friend. Rest and have peace within your soul."

Rappahanock blew a heavy breath over Hyde which sent the otter into a deep sleep. With one paw behind his head, Rappahanock lowered his friend back in his chair to let him rest. His prayer stick was attached to a long necklace that was draped around the bear's neck. Taking it in his paw, Rappahanock began to pray.

"Almighty," he said. "Meet this young one in his dreams. Speak to his soul and revive his spirit. I am not sure of tomorrow, but, here and now I ask you to set Your words deep inside of him; that he would walk according to Your ways." Rappahanock got a feeling and stopped praying. He sensed the Almighty conversing with him. His head lifted and he looked to the center table where they had shared their meal earlier.

Rappahanock walked over to the table and found two new candles. He used a dying candle to light the new, then he pressed the bottom of the new candle on to the tops of the old. The hot, soft, wax melded with the cold, hard, wax; making almost a stand from the prior. He did likewise with the other.

"Hmmm," he said to himself. Though he asked the Almighty, "It will be the second generation?"

The candles flame flickered.

"The second generation of Hyde will carry his flame and be propped up like so?" he asked.

The flames from the candles, simultaneously, blew out and gave off two puffs of smoke; each writing a unique word. The one wrote "Stone" while the other wrote "paw." Once he saw the words, Rappahanock shook awake in his armchair. Some time had passed, but had it been a dream? He looked left and right to see all of Toppehan at rest, even the fire in its place was burning low.

He leaned forward and placed some new logs on the fire. He took a long stick and stoked the embers below to bring the fire back to life. He cozied up in his armchair once more and leaned back, though his eyes never left the fire. He let the words roll around his muzzle as he pondered the dream. "Stone," he said. "Paw. Hmmm. Stone. Paw." Past Rappahanock's shoulder two candles, half burned, flickered and danced in the quiet hall of Toppehan.

8

The night clung to the horizon as bears and otters lined the bank of the Chessa. Another few hours had passed since Rappahanock stirred in the night. Though, now was the time for Hyde and his beasts to paddle southward in order to arrive and ascend the hill of the Crown by dawn. Breathing in deep, Rappahanock searched the early morning air with his nose; sniffing as he breathed in and out.

The great bear said, "Hyde. Our prayer will be this:

> Through the dark hours of this night
> protect and surround us,
> Almighty, in all of Your forms.
> Forgive the ill that we have done.
> Forgive the pride that we have shown.
> Forgive the words that have caused harm
> that we might sleep peaceably,
> and rise refreshed to do your will.
> Through the dark hours of this night
> protect and surround us,
> Almighty, in all of Your forms.

"And for your warriors, my prayer is this:

This night and every night
grant light.
This night and every night
grant peace.
This night and every night
grant rest.
This night and every night
grant grace.
This night and every night
grant joy.

"In the name of the Almighty, we pray these things," said Rappahanock, ending his discourse with Hyde and his followers. "I pray that we shall see one another again, soon," added Hyde, out of formality but having forgotten their last conversation due to that late hour.

Rappahanock smiled and added, "Me too, my old friend. Whether in this life or the next."

Hyde replied in kind, "Whether in this life or the next." The two friends clasped paws once more and hugged one another. With a flick of his muzzle Hyde ordered Ptero to load everyone into the boats. Swiftly they moved, into the boats and out onto the water.

As they shoved off, the great bear raised his prayer stick once more, and said, "May the Realm be with you. And Hyde, remember," tugging on the handle of his prayer stick Rappahanock removed a hidden blade, "not all prayers are passive."

Hyde raised a paw in return to bid farewell to his good friend as paddles were placed to water. The otters continued their course upriver, now under a more peaceful yet cautious perspective.

Hyde cherished the gentle wisdom of Rappahanock. For many moons they shared counsel and friendship with one another; the Almighty always being first and foremost among their thoughts and conversations. As the canoes paddled away the sea otter massaged an old scar on his left shoulder, though hidden beneath his furry exterior. Hyde was not only massaging the wound but the memory of how he managed to survive that particular battle. Turning around to see his rescuer, Rappahanock was nowhere to be seen. The otter snickered to himself.

Ptero asked, "Chief?"

"Remember'n," replied Hyde, "just ... remember'n."

"He's a wise one, that bear," added Ptero.

"Ay, he is that," said Hyde.

"What of our ascent?" asked Ptero.

"Rappahanock is not one to give warning idly," answered Hyde. "Let's see the hour upon which we arrive at the plains of Boulder. Until then, let's keep our wits about us."

"Ay," said Ptero.

From the woodland cover Rappahanock watched the otters glide out of sight. Lowering his head, he smiled and continued on back to the oak, though the smile slowly disappeared with every step he took. Clutching his prayer stick tightly in his paw, he paused a moment in the middle of the wood and said, "Keep them and guide them. And more than that ..." The great bear shook his head and stopped. He continued by saying, "I fear that my very words may have the power to put things in motion that are still uncertain. So, I will only say, keep them and guide them." He simply clutched his prayer stick tighter and walked on toward Toppehan.

9

As time crept slowly towards dawn, Draven stepped into the Crown, light flickering off of the candles on the windowsill where Canis and Lupus were sitting. The sun was just beginning to send its yellow glow over the edge of the horizon in the east, though it had not yet risen. The alpha wolf caught sight of Draven and nodded for the young wolf to approach. Canis said, "When?"

Draven replied, "They haven't made the plains yet, so they must have stopped somewhere in the wood. Our ..." Draven was interrupted by a coyote, named Lani, who whispered in his ear. Draven listened intently, nodded, and said, "Canis. They've cleared the ford and are on the Cerulean."

"They're still on the river?" asked Canis.

Draven looked to Lani, who nodded "yes."

"They'll beach their boats soon," replied Canis. Turning his attention to his daughter, Canis said, "Lupus, what should we do?"

Lupus thought for a moment, then said, "You're still the alpha, father. What do you think we should do?"

Canis smiled, and replied, "We have two options. One, we light torches all around the Crown to let them know we're here while they're a ways off, or two, we keep things dark to keep them on their claws. Which would you choose?" Before Lupus could decline the decision, Canis added, "You have to choose one."

She smiled, knowing which option her father would choose. Then Lupus said, "I'd light the torches."

With a bit of a scowl, Canis asked, "Why?"

"Or ..." Lupus replied, but Canis cut her off.

"Daughter," he said, "as alpha, you will make decisions; not based off of the reactions of others, but upon your own response from within. When you speak, it happens. So, speak plain and speak firm."

"Well, it's hard to do that when you're sitting there staring at me!" she replied.

Canis laughed aloud and said, "Would it be better for me to look this way?" The alpha male turned his head upward to the magnificently vaulted room as if to howl to the ceiling. He and Lupus busted out into laughter.

"Thank you," she said. "Draven, light torches around the Crown. Let our guests know we're here and they are welcome."
Draven gave a brief bow to Canis and Lupus, then he and Lani made their exit to accomplish their task. Lupus turned to her father, "Was that the right decision, father?"

"Yes," said Canis. "But one thing you must remember, if you show weakness as the alpha, it invites any and all to challenge your authority. No one should back you down when it comes to your voice. It must be strong and sustained. Even if it's the wrong choice, you must never back down."

"Yes sir," said Lupus. "You mean like this?" The female wolf reared her head upward, as her father did before, and howled to the ceiling. They both burst into laughter and howled in the grand echo of the Crown.

As they settled down, Canis said, "But what do I know?" He shook his head with a sarcastic chuckle. "The way I've led was based on what my father taught me. You'll be the first female alpha since the days of Reffta. My grandfather said she was responsible for both strengthening Cahn and destroying it."

"Destroying it?" Lupus asked.

"She was the one who sought the borders of Cahn," replied Canis. "The maps we now have are thanks to her ..."

"So, the war with Chordatta," said Lupus, with a sense of revelation, "was also her doing."

Nodding his head, Canis said, "It changed everything. We've been at war ever since. Her legacy began with expanse, but it ended in war. Her great great grandpup, my great grandfather Rolop, was the one who finally drove the westerners back, so he was labeled the hero of Cahn. His son, Nida, was the one who began the war with the otters. Funny how the things we do in life follow us even in death."

"But the things that we're remembered for are the things that last," said Lupus. "You'll be remembered for uniting Cahn, just as your great grandfather was known as its hero."

Smiling, Canis said, "I pray that's enough to be remembered for, and not the countless lives I've taken."

"As alpha," said Lupus, "I'll make it so; you will be remembered for what takes place here today."

"And not as the otters call me?" asked Canis.

Lupus laughed and said, "I don't know what you mean, father."

"Sure, you don't," said Canis, with a shake of his head.

The two wolves nudged heads. Canis rubbing a paw on the back of his daughter's neck. Then she whispered, "Land orca."

"Liar!" said Canis. As he tussled her head.

"So, how do you know all this?" asked Lupus.

"About being called land orca?" asked Canis.

"No," laughed Lupus, "about our history."

"As alpha," replied Canis, "you'll have access to the ancient scrolls of Cahn. They're kept in a cave at the base of Shausta. When we return, I will show you."

From outside the door, Grolg watched his father and sister sit on the windowsill as they nuzzled and laughed together. He clenched his jaw and his nostrils flared as his inner rage boiled. His eyes hardened. His hair stood on edge as he felt threatened, exposed. The young wolf stomped off, growling to himself.

Grolg ended up back on his perch as he looked down over the country south and east of Boulder. The night's grip was all but spent, as the moon and stars lost their shine to the greater light that broke forth over Cahn. The Cerulean River shimmered reflections of the last celestial hosts as it carried it's fresh mountain water downstream toward the River Phire. Just beyond the river, Grolg saw a small party of beasts beach their canoes and gather along the river's edge. With a cold tone he said to himself, "What a shame if they all ended up dead."

10

The sun's first shades of light poured over the edge of the horizon, shades of pink and orange scattered everywhere with great anticipation. Birds chirped. Insects sang.

Hyde hicked a hind paw up onto the first exposed rock he came to. They had reached Boulder by dawn, now Hyde and his warriors were ready to climb. He squinted his eyes as he looked up the gradual grade toward the Crown. Checking his flint stock and powder, he nodded for the others to follow suit. Rifles were loaded and blades were checked and sharpened.

Ptero gave Hyde a funny look, to which the seasoned sea otter replied, "It may be just a dark cloud, so to speak, but that doesn't mean we're just go'n ta roll over and get rained on." A mischievous smile sprung upon every face.

Ptero said, "Ya hear that boys? We're go'n dance'n in the rain!"

Everyone chuckled. Hyde turned around and held up his paws for attention. It was no longer time for smiles. He raised three claws and pointed for three of his otters and said, "You three follow Mik up the right side." Three claws again, he pointed for three others and said, "You three go with Slate up the left." Lowering four claws, he wiggled them and said, "The rest of you follow me." With a nod the warrior chieftain turned and started the climb.

His warriors did as they were told. The climb started out easy enough, but as the rocks grew larger and more jagged, they were forced to either climb up or hike around certain spots. Their pace slowed, but their eyes were keen and their ears were perked.

Up above Grolg watched as they ascended to the peak. He counted the otters' numbers and noted their positions. He turned and hurried to the Crown in order to make his report to Canis. Grolg said to himself, "Once Canis knows they're set to fight, he'll understand there's no such thing as peace with water trash."

Bursting into the great hall of Boulder, Grolg bellowed, "Father! Your friend, the otter, is on this way."

Canis spun around at the sound of his son. "Good," replied Canis, as he dipped his paws into a bowl of cool water, "let's go and meet him." The alpha wolf washed his face, took his towel and dried himself. Lupus did likewise as they freshened up from the long night.

"They've taken tactical positions and are ascending the slope all spread out," said Grolg, "as if they're hoping to engage. We must fight back!"

"Grolg," said Canis, as Lupus grabbed the cloth to dry her paws, "I wouldn't trust an otter's word any more than they trust mine. We have to show ourselves peaceful if we wish them to be peaceable."

"Are you mad?" Grolg howled. "Have you lost your mind! These otters are the ones who've taken everything from us!"

"Everything?" Canis said, calmly. "What about me? What about your sister? Would you endanger us in order to have your taste for blood? Or are you so blinded by grief that you cannot see what you've become?"

Not expecting an answer, Grolg asked dismissively, "Oh? And what's that, father?"

"Me," said Canis.

Grolg was thrown off by the idea. He shook it from his mind and said, "I haven't become like you. You're half the wolf you used to be! If this is who you've become, then you've failed as alpha!"

"No son," replied Canis, "Up until now I have failed as alpha. I put my own greed before the needs of every land dog that we've lost. I was just too blind to see it until now." Grolg scoffed at the notion, but Canis added, "and I've been too blind to see that I've failed you son ..."

Grolg backed away from Canis, "What? How have you failed me?"

"By teaching you that the only way to rule is to destroy," said Canis. "Don't become like me son. Be better than me. Come with us. Join us as we end this bloody war and walk with us into the new Cahn. A united Cahn. A stronger Cahn. One led by Lupus!"

Draven called in from beyond the Crown, "They're on their way."

Turning to the door Canis invited his children to walk with him. Lupus joined him, but Grolg just stood there. The young wolf was perplexed beyond repair. Within him two wolves were at war. One wolf was tired and ready to hang up his knives and axes, the other was a coal from a fire; grey on the outside but burning hotter than a forge within. He started to breathe heavily and uncontrollably. Slowly the tired wolf was gone while the other wolf, that was now given a little oxygen, burst into flames.

As Canis and Lupus exited the Crown, Grolg turned toward the door. He unsheathed his knife and ax from his belt. He gripped them so tightly his arms began to shake, then his whole body. He worked himself up into a rage. When he finally hit the melting point, he howled like a mad beast "Her?! You'd ordain her?! Over me??" He sprinted out of the great hall and followed after his sister. When he rounded the corner everything paused for a moment.

Lupus looked over her shoulder to wave him on. Canis was lifting his paws in the air to receive Hyde and his fellow otters. Draven looked up to see Grolg closing in on the alpha. With the full strength of a viper, Grolg coiled himself up and sprang into the air to pounce on Canis. His blades raised, body coiled, Grolg meant to drive a crushing blow into his father's back.

11

*H*yde held up a paw, "Hold!" Trying to get a better look, he said, "What happened ta Canis?"

Ptero said, "Looks like he took behind that rock."

Hyde said, "Keep a keen eye. We're not out of the woods yet."

Further up the hill, Grolg stood to his paws. He snarled at the bloodied body of the grey wolf laying before him, but the euphoria was wrenched from his face as he watched Canis stand to his paws. "But I," he said. "You ... I ... But ..."

Lupus had jumped in between her brother and father, taking the full weight of Grolg's fury. The knife and axe were buried into her fur when the three wolves rolled to the ground.

Falling to his knees, Canis tried to wrapped Lupus in his arms, but he couldn't for the pain it would cause. He lifted his head and howled. He cupped her head in his paws and said to her, "Lupus! Baby! Stay with me!" As Draven came to aid the fallen maiden a switch snapped in Canis' brain. He looked up into Grolg's eyes, but not as he did before. There were no longer fond expressions of peace, no more talk of better days; the wolf that Canis had been fighting back into the recesses of his soul came bounding out of him with the wind speed of a tornado. He shook uncontrollably as he howled, "What have you done?! You mean to murder me? In cold blood?"

Canis exploded off the ground and was upon Grolg before the young wolf could take a step. Canis swung and punched Grolg in the jaw, knocking him to the left, but another paw was already flying, knocking Grolg to the right. Canis hit his son so many times that Grolg had no way to catch his balance. An uppercut caused Grolg to bend back and then bow before his father, then Canis raised his paws up above his head and drove down onto Grolg's skull. Grolg hit the dirt, and Canis was on him. Drawing his axe high, Canis raised the blade up above his head, his son was no longer; he meant to bury the axe deep into the beast before him.

Lupus growled, "Father, no!" As best she could, she tried to call out again through the pain and hoarseness of breath, "Father! Don't kill him!" Canis was caught in some kind of blood fog, but Lupus tried once more. She remembered what her mother used to say in times like this. Lupus reared up as best she could and said, "Eagle Eye ... Eikeli!"

The alpha's arms froze. His axe was poised to kill, but the familiar phrase stayed his weapon, instantly drawing tears to his eyes. He said to himself, "I haven't ... since ... Nuppella ..." His paws flung open and the axe fell to the ground. In like fashion Canis buckled and fell to his knees, tears streaming from his eyes as his paws quaked in front of him.

"Look!" he shouted at his son. "Look what we become when blood is all we seek! Blood for blood! Is that what you want? Then here," he said, lifting his chin and exposing his neck, "take your blood and be done with it!"

With his eyes closed, the alpha offered up his life; right into his son's paws but Grolg was still disoriented from the beating he'd received. After a few moments, where nothing had happened, Canis turned around and began to crawl on all fours towards his daughter; he repeated the phrase softly, "Eikeli. Eikeli."

As he approached Lupus, Hyde and his otters came up the other side of the hill. Upon seeing Lupus, with the ax and knife still in her back, they approached her with weapons lowered and paws held high, in order to lend aid. They reached her the same time Canis did.

"What happened?" asked Hyde.

Canis shook his head, he could only reply, "Eikeli."

"How can we help?" Hyde asked Draven.

"You can ..." Draven began to reply, but the words were cut from his mouth as a blade flew by his head and buried itself into the otter chieftain's chest. Hyde stumbled backward. The alpha wolf roared as he spun around to see Grolg, feebly, standing on his hind legs; a sinister smile running across his face.

"Close enough," said Grolg. He'd missed Canis, but Hyde would do.

Ptero raised his rifle to fire upon him.

Boom

Canis had reached out and took the otter's rifle in his paw just before Ptero fired, diverting the shot, as the smoke billowed from the barrel. The rifle round tore through the right side of Grolg's neck; knocking him back.

"Run!" howled Canis. Grolg managed to hobble his way toward the boulders behind him in order to escape, clasping a paw over his oozing wound. Ptero unsheathed his hatchet and moved to follow Grolg but Canis stood out in front of him.

"Get out of me way, Canis," said Ptero as he shoved Canis.

Canis raised his paws and stood in Ptero's way, while he said, "He's my cub."

"I do'na care," barked Ptero.

Canis replied, "I know. I know. Tend to your chieftain. I'll take care of that welp."

Hyde managed to whisper and say, "Canis."

The alpha wolf hurried to Hyde's side and knelt beside the otter chieftain, "Hyde."

"Liar ..." uttered Hyde, through whistling breaths.

"Hyde," said Canis, "I never ..."

Hyde sneaked out another word, "Why?"

"Why did I ask you here?" asked Canis. Hyde nodded and the wolf said, "I asked you here that we might take one another's paw in peace and end this bloodshed. So, that Cahn might be united once more."

"Land and water," replied Hyde, with a brief smile.

"Exactly," said Canis.

"Here," said Hyde, as he reached into his shirt, "take this." Mustering up what strength he had left, the sea otter said, "Give it to me daughter, Lutris, so she can see it and know that this is me, final bid'n. Ta unite the dogs." Hyde coughed. Blood spurted from his mouth. He managed to add one last thing by saying, "Let her know you give this ta her in order that she may see that her father died in peace, seeking peace and at peace with you, Canis, by my side. Give it to her that she may rule Cahn."

"I'll do just that," said Canis, taking Hyde's paw in his own as they both clasped the blue sapphire Paragon. With that Hyde breathed his last. Canis closed Hyde's eyes, lowered his paw and took the Cerulean in his own.

Being just a few boulders away Lutris charged up the hill. She only saw Hyde on the ground and Canis standing to his paws over him, but the sight of the Cerulean in Canis' paw sent a wavering bolt of lightning through her spine. Her ears rang, her eyes ran red and her soul was on fire.

As she ascended the hill, Canis caught sight of her out of the corner of his eye. He lifted his paws to greet her, but the sight of her rifle raised caused him to cower. Ptero raised his paws to stop her, but it was too late.

Boom

The rifle round hit Canis in the shoulder, flinging him back and to the left. Lutris dropped her rifle and brandished her knife and hatchet.

"Lu! It's not what it seems!" said Ptero, him and the other otters tried to stop her, but it was like trying to stop a wave from crashing on the sand. She broke through their ranks and lunged toward Canis. He managed to pick up a knife from the ground and tried his best to perry the onslaught of blows coming from the enraged female otter; but Lutris drove him back step after step.

"Lutris!" he shouted, but she didn't hear him. "Hyde gave it me!" Canis tried once more, but the deeper rage of the otter only saw red.

As Lutris attacked Canis she bellowed a fearsome roar, "Ahhhh!" Tears streaming from her eyes, foam frothing from her mouth. She swung time and time again at the wolf with all her might. Canis dodged and repelled what attacks he could, but the rage of the otter maid was too much. She reared back and kicked him in the gut. Breath went flying from the Alpha's mouth. It was in that moment that he knew there was no escaping her vengeance. So, he let down his knife and with that she kicked him to the ground.

He looked up at her and said, "Strike me down! Strike me down for Hyde!"

"Don't you ..." Lutris couldn't even get the words out past her anger and tears. She leapt onto Canis and exacted her revenge for her fallen father.

She watched Canis breath his last. As he did he managed to whisper, "Eikeli ..."

After retrieving the Cerulean from the ground, Lutris stood to her paws. She slowly walked over to her father and fell on him, weeping as she embraced him.

Just beyond reach, Ptero stood with Dyrk and the other otters. Tobias came running toward the scene, only to see his niece sobbing over the fallen form of his brother. He knelt next to him and placed a paw on Hyde's shoulder, gripping his kin's hat in his other paw.

Ptero was in absolute shock. His friend and chieftain lay in the dirt while he was still standing. He whispered to himself, "I've failed you."

There's an old saying among otters, so that grief can be expressed, that goes as follows:

"Ne'er try ta stop the flow, Of water on an otter's coat
Waterways both in and on, Can ne'er stop once they begin"

25th Age

of

Cahn

Two seasons later ...

12

The fire crackled and danced as Lutris held her four week old pup who cooed and yawned like only a pup can. Dyrk looked over her shoulder and into the fierce blue eyes of their son. He said, "My, he's the spittin' image of ya, hun."

"He takes after Hyde," replied Lutris, "and a bit of you."

"That's pure sea otter right there, Lu," said Dyrk.

"Well," said Lutris, with a sigh, "he may have me family's looks, but he has your scowl!"

The two otters laughed and nudged heads, as Dyrk said, "River otters don't scowl. We're just ..."

"Bull headed?" answered Tobias, as he approached the young family.

"Aye, Uncle," said Lutris, as she chuckled. "Quite bull-headed."

"Bull-headed?" scoffed Dyrk. "I've never been more known than at this very moment!" Laughter surrounded them as the elder sea otter leaned over Lutris' other shoulder to peer down on the young pup.

"Spittin' image of Hyde," said Tobias.

"Ay," replied Dyrk, "I was just sayin' the same."

Lutris cut her eyes at her husband, to which the wise river otter leaned down and kissed her on the brow. She smiled and nudged his head once more. Turning her attention to Tobias, she asked, "What brings ya over this way tonight?"

"I can'na come see me own great nephew?" asked Tobias.

"You can!" answered Lutris, "And you have every night this week, but not nearly as dressed as ya are!"

Tobias backed up and looked at himself with his arms akimbo, "I guess me colors do give me away." Tobias' typical flowing shirt was adorned with his tribe's sash and knee-high kilt, the colors weaved of green and deep blue that matched his blue tam-o-shanter; which was tilted ever so slightly over the right side of his head. Three feathers were pinned to his hat by an old sea shell and another shell of greater size buckled his belt across his waist. His bracelets, of varying sizes, rolled up both arms and the Cerulean hung about his neck from a golden chain.

The elder otter cleared his throat and said, "With your permission, Lutris and Dyrk, I would like to call the elders together for a ceremony." The two otters nodded in reply, to which Tobias raised his conch shell and gave it a blow.

Wooohrrrrr

From beyond the shadows of the fire eleven otters stepped forward. Sea, river and giant otters alike, adorned in their tribes' festive colors, formed a circle around the family. Tobias laid his conch shell on the ground and drew a short sword from its sheath. The other otters did likewise. Tobias said, "Dyrk! Will you vow to protect this pup? Will you vow to provide for this pup? Will you vow to present this pup as an upstanding otter among otters? For he is of the bloodline of Lutris and Hyde before her and Hars before him. Will you vow to bring up this pup in the way he should go?"

Dyrk, through tears, nodded and said, "Ay. I do so vow."

Twelve swords gently descended upon the river otters' shoulders. Twelve elders acknowledged the pledge that was made and in so doing they, ceremonially, let Dyrk know that their swords were his swords and his family's swords.

Tobias cleared his throat once more, "Lutris! Chieftess of the northern region of Cahn. Will you vow to nurture this pup? Will you vow to love this pup? Will you vow to present this pup as an upstanding otter among otters? For he is of your bloodline and those who had begat you. Will you vow to establish this young pup as a ruler of otters and a servant of all?"

Lutris wiped away tears of her own and said, "Ay. I do so vow."

Each elder took their turn to stand in front of Lutris, and knelt with their sword tip in the ground, holding the hilt of their swords with both paws. Twelve knees bowed and twelve swords dug into the ground, ceremonially, to make it known that they have offered their very lives to protect the life of this mother and pup.

Clearing his voice once more, Tobias laughed and said, "Sorry. These fits of coughing keep coming. I may need to cut the pipe a time or two to get this throat settled." The otters snickered, but tried to keep straight faces. Clearing his throat once more, Tobias said, "May I see the lad?" Lutris nodded to which Tobias took the young otter into his paws.

"Elders," said Tobias, "will you vow to guide this pup? Will you vow to encourage and train up this pup? Will you vow to present this pup as an upstanding otter among otters? For he is of the original bloodline of Lutris, our chieftess. Will you vow to keep this pup in the corner of your eye at all times?"

Each elder stepped forward and placed a paw on the young otters head and said, "Ay. I do so vow."

Raising the boy in the air, Tobias said with a strong voice, "Here is Stonepaw! Heir to the rule of Cahn, heir of the Cerulean and son of the tribes of Lutris!"

"Ahh Ooo," replied the elders. With that, the ceremony was over, and the feasting was just about to begin.

Tobias lowered Stonepaw and returned him to his mother and father. He said, "This pup is go'n ta change the world!"

"We know!" replied Lutris.

"Ah," said Tobias, as he spotted Ptero just beyond the group of elders, "come, T."

Ptero stepped forward. His kit was frayed but clean. He laid his weapons at Lutris and Stonepaw's feet and bowed low. Lutris placed a paw on the guards shoulder to which Ptero sat back up; tears streaming down his face. He had not yet been able to approach Lutris since Hyde's death, feeling the full burden of responsibility. He said, through broken tones, "Though I do'na deserve an audience with you ..."

"Ptero!" said Lutris, kneeling down into the dirt with him, "I do'na hold you responsible."

"But I do!" said Ptero.

"There is no such claim," said Lutris, "from me nor anyone at Boulder that day. I trust you!"

Tears spilled out onto Ptero's cheeks as he heard what he longed to hear from his chieftess. He mustered up what strength he could to say, "I feel I must take a leave as chief guard for a season. Do you so release me?"

"As your chieftess," said Lutris, "I release you. Though, know you are welcome back any time."

Ptero nodded and began to rise, but he quickly knelt once more. He said, "Though I may'na be obliged to in this season, I vow ta protect you and this pup with me very life. I vow ta train Stonepaw as me very own and to show him the ways of our tribes and chieftains." Ptero paused and looked into Lutris' eyes, and said, "And if ever you need me know that your family and the tribes of Cahn have me."

"Thank you T," said Lutris. "I now have a greater understanding of why me father held you in such high esteem. You really are a noble otter of otters." With that Ptero nodded and slipped away.

Tobias watched as Ptero walked off into the darkness. He turned around to address the elders and said, "Come now! There's feasting to be done!"

Lutris and Dyrk laughed as the eleven hungry elders made their way to the tables for the celebratory meal. As they walked off one by one leaving Tobias with Stonepaw and his parents.

"Thank you uncle," said Lutris.

"My pleasure," said Tobias, though he stood there in a mild silence.

"What is it uncle?" asked Dyrk. "I thought you'd be the first after that pile of shrimp?"

"I wonder," said Tobias, "if I might have your permission once more."

"What is it, Tobias?" asked Lutris.

"Hyde was me brother," answered Tobias, "and it's

custom for the kin of the fallen to make certain concessions for the kin that are left behind ... if you follow me meaning."

"Are you ...?" asked Lutris, but Tobias took the words out of her mouth.

"I'd like," said Tobias, "with your permission of course, to adopt you as me own daughter; making Stonepaw, here, me own grandpup."

Lutris leapt and hugged Tobias, saying, "Nothing would make me happier."

"Do we need to call the elders back?" asked Dyrk, as he reached down for the conch shell.

"I don't think so," said Tobias. "We can do this one ourselves here before the Almighty. And then we'll feast as a family! Would you retrieve Wode? He's a part of this too."

"Let me get him," said Dyrk as he entered his tent. Once he returned to the fire, they began.

Tobias prayed the prayer of the otters when adopting one, or more, as their own. The five of them stood there, under the eyes of the Almighty and vowed a family's prayer over one another and the boys. That was the night Tobias took Lutris and her family under his watchful eye, which would turn out to be the beginning of a long and legendary journey.

"Thank you gran." said Lutris.

"Gran?" said Tobias. "I think I like the sound of that."

"Well get used to it," laughed Lutris. "Now, where are those shrimp? I'm starving!"

13

The night continued on. Candles were lit. Tables were dressed. Kegs were tapped. All manner of sea food was available at every station: shrimp, crab, lobster, flounder, tuna and all other manner of aquatic fare. Otters everywhere were dressed in their best tribal colors; dancing, laughing and feasting. Music was played on stringed and wind instruments, driven with tribal drums.

Tobias looked up and called out, saying, "Rappahanock! Zon Tidea! What kept ya?"

Zon Tidea, a quiet and awkward sort of porcupine, stepped forward. He was dressed in meager trappings; a loose shirt, that his back quills poked out of, and a loin cloth. Though he carried a stout walking stick painted and carved in the porcupine way. He took another step forward and said, in a broken kind of meter, "Thank you ... for ... inviting me ... to ... this ... celebration. I've had ... some of my kin ... bring Boulder Gold ... for the party. Please, drink and ... be merry!"

Tobias needed no second bidding. He grabbed a bottle and uncorked the golden bourbon, which was paw-crafted by the porcupines in the Boulder wood. Tobias said, "You were welcome before you armed me with this stuff! Now you'll be invited to all of our festivities from now on!"

Lutris bowed elegantly before the master of porcupines and said, "Thank you for celebrating our son with us!" Zon Tidea bowed in kind and awkwardly stepped back.

Dyrk said, "And who's this?"

The porcupine and bear stepped aside to reveal a scrawny, but able-bodied young squirrel. He was adorned with a robe of wolf's fur and his headdress boasted of different types of feathers. A necklace of canine claws hng from his thin neck. He stepped forward and cleared his throat while he waited to be introduced. Rappahanock said, "My apologies. Allow me to introduce Delmarv, the new chieftain of the western wood."

Delmarv bowed his head slightly and looked over at Stonepaw. "This is who we've come to celebrate?" he said. Lutris looked Delmarv in the eye and said, "This is my son, Stonepaw."

Delmarv bowed once more and said, "I look forward to when he's grown." With a grimace look, the squirrel bowed one last time and walked away.

The great bear stepped forward and knelt gracefully before Lutris and her family. He clasped her paw in his own and, looking up into her eyes, said, "Blessings over you and your beautiful pup! May I see him?" Lutris nodded, allowing Rappahanock to hold her son. Looking down on the young otter, he said, "My. He has Hyde's appearance! Tell me, what was his name again?"

"Stonepaw," replied Lutris.

The name rolled around Rappahanock's soul and heart as he searched his memory. He kept saying, "Stonepaw? Stonepaw?"

"What is it, Rappahanock?" asked Lutris.

"There's just something about that name?" replied the bear. "Once it comes to me I will let you know." Looking down into the otter's eyes, Rappahanock said, "Stonepaw. I see such greatness in you. You will truly be one to change the world! Your journey will take you round it time and time again, but your purpose in Cahn has yet to be decided! I look forward to seeing what type of otter you will become!" He paused a moment. Then he said, "I feel I have more to say, but until I understand why this name is sticking in my heart I shall wait to share more at another time."

Lutris smiled as Rappahanock returned her son. The great bear walked away still whispering the name, "Stonepaw ... Stonepaw ..."

"Rapp!" whispered Tobias. The bear was rattled for a moment as he was still deep in thought over the pup's name. So, Tobias whispered again, "Rappahanock!"

The second call shook the bear from his trans. He turned and smiled, saying, "Tobias! Come, let us feast and drink in honor of the fallen, Hyde!"

"Aye," replied Tobias, "we'll do just tha'. Have you heard anythin'?"

The look of concern on the otter's face drew Rappahanocks suspicions to one name, "Grolg?" he asked.

"Aye," replied Tobias.

"I wish him dead for what he did but for all we know, he is alive," said Rappahanock, "though that is all we know. There are scouts spread across the belt of Cahn from Toppehan to Boulder and beyond into Delmarv's territory. Not one beast has seen or heard from anyone who's seen that grey, murderous, canine."

"Perhaps Ptero's rifle round turn'd infectious?" asked Tobias.

"The wolves have strong medicine," answered the bear. "They've always been attuned to the earth and her secrets. Though I fear that they've begun to dabble in eastern medicines which could not only heal Grolg but twist him and turn him even worse. I fear a greater power is at work here in Cahn. Canis sought to resist it. It feels like Grolg is seeking it." Rappahanock paused a moment, then he realized that he was speaking his thoughts and that they had brought more concern to Tobias.

He put on a quick smile and patted his friend on the shoulder, saying "But that's merely bear talk. I fear that my hunger has made me suspicious! I've been fasting all day in anticipation for this feast! Come my friend!"

The two friends walked toward the fire and tables in order to join the others in their merriment.

The party went on into the night. Fires were kept high; tables were stocked well and laughter was in right supply.

Once the food was eaten and the drinks were drunk and stories were remembered, one by one otters and the like made their retreat to bed. As the night came to a close, Tobias returned the Cerulean to Lutris. She looped the necklace around Stonepaw's neck and said, "This will be yours soon enough."

Tobias returned to his own tent and began making preparations to move his things and belongings closer to Lutris' as was custom for adoption.

Back in their own tent, Lutris and Dyrk laid Stonepaw down on his pallet of pillows next to the sleeping Wode.

Lutris prepared herself to climb into bed but noticed Dyrk reaching for his rifle. "Dyrk?"

"Nightly checks," said Dyrk. "Be back in a tick."

"We have others to look in on such things," replied Lutris, with a roll of her eyes.

"Aye," said Dyrk, "and aren't I just the beast you ordered?"

"We'll be asleep by the time you get back," said Lutris, "but kiss me goodnight when you come in."

"Of course, me dear," said Dyrk. He planted a kiss on her forehead, and another on Stonepaw's and Wode's. He looked down on his sons and said, "So drastically different, yet they carry so much strength!"

"Aye," said Lutris, "our sweet boys."
Dyrk caressed both of his sons heads, then he exited their tent and went on his way. Lutris blew out the candle and sunk down in bed a skip away from her pups.

Outside the coast was clear. Otters everywhere were settled in for the night, save those on watch. As Dyrk went to check the other sentries scattered across the army's camp, there were two guards left outside of the chieftess' tent to stand guard in the quiet, hushed, hours of night.

The fire still crackled and moaned, disguising the paw steps of those sneaking up behind them. A twig broke behind one of the otter guards. Before he could turn round to see if anybeast was there a paw wrapped around his mouth and a dagger was thrust into his neck.

The cloaked beast dragged the body behind the tent while others snuck up on the second guard. He was dealt with in like fashion. A quick whistle called the 'all clear' and a pack of wolves stepped out from the edge of the wood and approached the campsite.

Grolg was the last to step forward. The wound on his neck still smelled of rotted flesh, but it wasn't enough to take the new alpha down, nor would he let it. He tenderly played with the leaves that were tied to his neck. Thanks to a potent mixture of aloe, lavender and willow sap, along with some other elixirs, the new alpha of Cahn was on the mend.

Grolg had told the whole of Canis' hordes how the otters descended on Boulder and killed Canis and Lupus. He nearly escaped with his life; so he said. Some didn't believe the young wolf's story but because of the wound and the death of Canis and Lupus the beta pack leaders had to submit to Grolg's authority; not to mention the absolute rage it sent the rest of the lesser pack leaders into, most of which were allies of Grolg. He called for retaliation. Had any canine opposed the new alpha it would certainly have ended in blood.

Back at the campsite, stood a hooded wolf, Creed, one of Canis' most trusted beta wolves. Creed was a sullen wolf; never outspoken but keen and attentive. He served Canis well in being around conversations but not being recognized. Most of the other wolves in the beta pack didn't pay Creed much attention which made him a valuable asset and spy for the new alpha. He stepped close to Grolg and said, "Are you sure we should be doing this?"

"Of course!" whispered Grolg, through a gravelly voice as the pain of his neck pulsed, "she's the very beast that killed our beloved alpha! My father!"

Another stepped forward, Pfank. He was a lesser wolf in the beta order, but he realized that in this transition of power that position was everything. He had been priming Grolg to become alpha for the last few seasons, and now that Grolg had assumed authority Pfank took his chance to be a mentor and voice. He pushed his own agenda all under the guise of what was best for Grolg and the wolf nation. He pounded his paw and said, "It is right that Grolg seek vengeance on her who took his father and sister from him!"

Grolg replied to those with him, saying, "The pack elders agreed. An eye for an eye!"

A snarly toothed canine, named Orpheus, leaned in and said, with a laugh, "Or a f'roat for a f'roat!"

Pfank leaned in and whispered in Grolg's ear, saying, "A throat indeed if you don't finish this like you promised to them elders!"

Grolg lifted his paws for everyone to stop. His elevated heart rate caused his neck to throb uncontrollably. Through coarse whispers, Grolg said, "No one enters." His canines nodded and stood guard as he gently pulled back on the flap of Lutris' tent and entered.

I 4

A beast came charging through the forest, to which Dyrk whispered sharply, "Get ready!"

Rappahanock came bounding up to the edge of the fire. Out of breath, the bear raved on and on about something or other. Dyrk tried to calm him down, "Whoa big fella. What's wrong? What's all this?"

"Stonepaw," said the bear. "Where is he? I need to see Stonepaw!"

"What for? You just saw him a few hours ago?" said Dyrk.

"He's the one!" growled Rappahanock.

"Yeah," said Dyrk, "we knew that. That's what the whole night was ..."

Rappahanock growled again, "Cause he's in danger!"

Dyrks paws swept him away before it dawned on the river otter what could be taking place. As he and Rappahanock turned the big pine they saw a group of wolves skulking around his tent. "No," he growled, as his paws were sped to his family. He cupped his conch shell and raised the alarm.

Woohhrrrrrr

"Whatever occurs," roared the great bear, "tend to your kin!"

The pair of warriors raced on into the night as the canines raised their heads to the night sky.

Creed raised his head and said, "They're coming."

Pfank called out, "Grolg! Get out of there!"

The curtain ripped open and a frazzled Grolg exited the tent, blood stained paws and a sack thrown over his shoulder. "Where? Where are they?"

"Here!" roared Rappahanock, as he swiped his massive paw at the first wolf he reached. The beast flew into the fire and screeched as his fur took flame. Dyrk, still a few steps behind the bear, raised his rifle and fired on a retreating Creed. The wolf spun violently from the lead ball that buried itself into his side. Scurrying up to his paws the wolf ran off into the night.

Rappahanock took after the wolves as they scattered like sheep in a tempest.

Meanwhile Dyrk's paws shook as he fell to his knees in the opening of the tent. His eyes transfixed on the bed. He slowly crawled over to the lifeless form of Lutris draped over the covers. As he approached her he tried to speak, but he couldn't. All he could do was keep his promise; so he planted a kiss on her forehead, climbed onto the bed and took her in his arms and held her. Tears lined his eyelids as his lip quivered viciously. He whispered to himself, "No' again."

When he looked upon her he noticed she wasn't under the sheets as he left her. "What were you doing ..." he began to ask, but his words trailed off as his eyes found the empty pallet with Stonepaw and Wode nowhere to be seen. Dyrk lowered Lutris to the bed and lept to the pallet of pillows. He pulled them away from the tent wall to see Wode huddled up in the corner.

"Almighty!" gasped Dyrk as he picked up his son.

Tobias entered the tent to see Dyrk and Wode holding each other. His eyes lifted and he saw his newly adopted daughter lifeless on the bed. Tobias shook the grief from his face and said quickly, "Here, let me have him. Tend to your bride."

Outside of the tent all manner of otters were gathered, having been drawn by the shell blast. Tobias exited the tent with his grandpup as Rappahanock stumbled back into the camp. The two found one another and Tobias asked, "What happened?"

"Grolg," said Rappahanock. An icy blast rolled off of the bears shoulders as he shook the thought from his own fur. "Lutris?"

The otter shook his head, signifying that she was gone but just then it dawned on him, Tobias said, "Where's Stonepaw?"

"The wolf had a sack over his shoulder when he departed the tent," growled Rappahanock. "I knocked him over in the woods, but when I rose to strike; I fell dark. Some beast must have hit me over the head for when I came to, they were gone."

"Are you say'n they took Stonepaw," asked Tobias.

"He tried," said Rappahanock, as he revealed the sack in question tucked in his left arm. Wrapped in it was Stonepaw, who was resting gently. "I found him in the sack a step away from where I fell. I must have knocked him loose when I hit Grolg."

"Thank the Almighty ... and thank you Rapp," said Tobias and gestured to hold Stonepaw.

Rappahanock passed the pup to Tobias, and the elder sea otter held both of his grandpups. Looking down on them both he noticed the Cerulean wasn't hanging around Stonepaw's neck. He brought the young sea otter close to nussle noses and said, "Glad you're safe and sound, me boy. Where's your necklace little one? I bet your mum put it back on before bed."

Looking up into the bears eyes, Tobias asked, "Do you think you killed him?"

"I'm not sure," said Rappahanock, "He cannot be feeling well at the moment."

Tobias nodded and moved to the fire. He found a stone, sat and rocked his two grandpups in the night as they gently rested. The sounds of grief echoing in everyone's ears as Dyrk made his long goodbyes.

Some hours later the flap swept open as Dyrk, with his bride draped across his arms, exited the tent. Every head held high, and every knee bent low. To see the fallen chieftess broke the heart of the tribes of Cahn. He approached Rappahanock and Tobias and said, "We must send her off ... to the counsel fire of the otters."

Down on the beach of Richmond, along the shore of the Chessa Bay, a boat was prepared. As was custom among the otter tribes of Cahn the boat was filled with pine branches and sap. Dyrk had wrapped her in burial cloth and the women and elders adorned her with wildflowers. Her bonet was laid on her chest, ringed in needles and thistles, while her weapons were laid at her side.

The old sea otter nudged his son-in-love and whispered, "Do you have the Cerulean?"

"No," said Dyrk. "Am I supposed t'?"

"Did'na Lutris have it on her?" asked Tobias.

"She did'na," replied Dyrk.

"She did'na?" asked Tobias.

"I thought she gave it to Stonepaw," said Dyrk. "Oh my, I nearly forgot! Where is ..."

"He's right here," said Tobias, "safe and sound."

"Oh, thank the Realm," said Dyrk, with a sigh of relief. "Does he not have it?"

"No," said Tobias, "he did'na have it on him."

Dyrk asked, "Where is it?"

Just then the elders came forward and picked up the boat, overhead, and began carrying Lutris through the masses toward the shore. Dyrk and Tobias followed them; Stonepaw and Wode in tow. The soft sands were lined with all manner of otters as Dyrk and Tobias said their final goodbyes. They stood to their paws, the elders eased the boat out into the gentle tide. They watched as she ebbed and flowed further into the moonlit bay.

Rappahanock stood next to Tobias. The old otter got his attention and whispered, "Did the boy have the Cerulean with him, when you found him?"

The bear shook his head and whispered back, "The stone is either in Grolg's paws or it's been lost to us." The two friends watched as the boat continued to carry away. Rappahanock finally said, "We will search the whole Cahn for it until it's found."

Tobias nodded, "Until it's found ... what hope do any of us have?"

When she was far enough off, a giant otter took his arrow to the fire, lifted it and took aim. He loosed the missile like a shooting star into the heavenly display. It rose and

fell on the floating pyre. Pipes swelled as the pine branches took flame. The otters on the shoreline shed their tears for their fallen chieftess as she lit up the waters around her. She joined the reflection of the night sky, becoming a burning star upon the sea.

Rappahanock lifted his prayer stick and said, "And so, we step out of the age of Lutris and into the age of Stonepaw. We return her to you, Almighty, as she was, a beacon of light." The boat continued to burn as it floated out of view.

About the Author and Series

If you enjoyed this book and would like to see the rest of the series become a reality, go to rekindleretreats.org/d-o-n-a-t-e to give towards the publishing of future stories.

All gifts are tax deductible.

For prints of Cerulean go to rekindleretreats.org/s-h-o-p to order a copy.

If you'd like to stay up to date with upcoming stories from The Legend of Evelyn go to rekindleretreats.org/s-h-o-p to subscribe to our *The Legend of Evelyn* email list.

C. J. Kuenzli works for Land of the Living, a 501(c)3 nonprofit ministry. All materials are created, published and printed through generous financial gifts under the stewardship of Land of the Living, their staff and board of directors. Their vision is to see generations restored to wholeness.

Through creative writing C. J. Kuenzli hopes to free minds and hearts to live from a place of true identity. The stories associated with The Legend of Evelyn are intended to unite the mind, soul and body to experience and hope for more!

The next story to be released from *The Legend of Evelyn* series is a full-length novel called: *Chickahominy*.